LITTLE HANDS CLAPPING

Also by Dan Rhodes

Anthropology
'A gleaming box of jazzy miniatures. Exquisitely funny.'
Guardian

Don't Tell Me The Truth About Love
'Bittersweet yet absurdly magical stories that will pull at your heart strings.
By forcing the hitherto unbelievable, it shows us an unknown world.'
The Times

Timoleon Vieta Come Home
'By turns hilarious and heart-rending. Rhodes is that real,
rare thing – a natural storyteller.'
Paul Bailey, *Sunday Times*

The Little White Car
(writing as Danuta de Rhodes)
'A cracking good read . . . enjoy yourself.'
Daily Express

Gold
Absolutely flawless . . . Fresh and funny.'
Observer

LITTLE HANDS CLAPPING

DAN RHODES

CANONGATE

Edinburgh · London · New York · Melbourne

Thanks to E. Rhodes, A-L. Sandstrum and S. L. Woods for
enduring early versions, F. Bickmore and all other Canongateers
past and present, Mazza's International Vulture Consultancy, Purvis
& Wade and the English teachers of Denmark for helping to keep
the wheels on the wagon, and, most of all, to Arthur.

The title is taken from Robert Browning's poem
The Pied Piper of Hamelin, and from the song
Little Hands by Alexander 'Skip' Spence.

This edition first published by Canongate Books in 2011

1

First published in Great Britain in 2010 by
Canongate Books Ltd, 14 High Street,
Edinburgh EH1 1TE

www.meetatthegate.com

British Library Cataloguing-in-Publication Data
A catalogue record for this book is available on
request from the British Library

ISBN 978 1 84767 530 9

Typeset in Plantin by Palimpsest Book Production Ltd,
Falkirk, Stirlingshire

Printed and bound in Great Britain by
Clays Ltd, St Ives plc

For Wife-features

PART ONE

I

At night, indeed at any time, but most of all at night, when the narrow street is lit only by the occasional lamp, there is little to distinguish the museum from the other buildings in the old part of the city. It is painted white, and rises three stories before tapering into a roof, where small windows jut from the immaculate tiles. It is set apart from its neighbours by the brass plate beside the door, which gives, in four languages, its name and the hours when its contents can be viewed. Only by standing close and squinting into the darkness is it possible to read the lettering, and as the first warm day of the year nears its end, nobody is taking the time to squint into the darkness. A small party of tourists passes by without paying the place any attention. They turn a corner, their voices fade, and the street is quiet until the next group comes along, young locals this time, their after-work drink having turned into a meal and several more drinks, their conversation reverberating from the high buildings as they head to somebody's apartment for a final glass.

The museum's lights are off, but that is not to say that the place is unoccupied. Behind one of the small windows sleeps an old man in a nightshirt and nightcap, their whiteness incandescent as it cuts through the dark. Partly covered by a single white sheet, and oblivious to the bursts of activity from the street below, he lies on a narrow bed. The skin of his face, a faint grey against the cotton that encases him, is a mosaic of oblongs, triangles and shapes without names. His mouth is open, his eyes are closed and the rattle of his breath fills the room. The old man is the museum's only resident, but this night he is not alone. The visitors are supposed to leave by five o'clock, but one had stayed on, huddling behind a large wooden display board as the door was bolted shut, and building up the courage to do what they had been meaning to do for so long. There are no sobs to be heard, and no wails. The visitor feels calm, and ready at last.

When this business is over and the story is out, or as much of the story as will ever be out, such interlopers will be described as having been drawn to the place *like moths to a flame*. While they are being counted and identified, articles will be written; some sober and balanced, others gleefully bug-eyed. None will capture the essence of the old man or even get a real grip on the events that had taken place under this roof. Nor will they convey any more than the haziest sense of the lives of these supposed moths, at least not what will often be referred to as their *inner lives* – the details beyond their education, employment history and haphazard lists of their likes and dislikes. With so little known about the thoughts and feelings from which they were built, these people will be presented to the world as having amounted to little more than a curriculum vitae, or a lonely hearts advertisement.

The more ambitious reporters will attempt to write something reflective, but frustrated by the incalculable blank spaces they will find their prose leaning towards the overwrought as they try, without much success, to make their way beneath the surface of the story. Their interviews with acknowledged experts will add nothing of interest to the copy, and references to Othello and Ophelia, Haemon and Antigone and the works of Émile Durkheim and David Hume will make them appear not so much learned as desperate. It is the tabloid writers who will be happiest, seasoning the facts with amateur psychological profiling, coarse conjecture and simple, alliterative blasts of moral condemnation as they pull together lurid account after lurid account.

Not wanting to know much beyond the basics,

most people will only read around the edges of these articles. Looking at the photographs they will begin, but no more, to imagine what must have been happening behind the eyes that sometimes stare back at them, and sometimes scowl, but more often than not smile.

At no stage will an editor allow an article to reach the press unless somewhere the people such as the one huddling behind the large display board are described as having been *like moths to a flame*. But if this place is a flame, it is a cold one. Even on a night like this the warmth has not penetrated the thick walls, and a wintry chill still pervades the building.

The last drunk of the night passes in the street, singing a song from generations ago, learned in childhood and never forgotten:

> *Frieda, oh Frieda,*
> *Will you still be mine*
> *When I am back from the war*
> *With a patch on my eye?*

It is supposed to be sung as a duet, but the drunk takes the woman's part too, a squawking, quavering parody of the female voice as she tells him that yes, of course she will still love him even though he has lost an eye.

Frieda, oh Frieda,
Will you still be mine
When I am back from the war
With my left arm torn off to the shoulder?

The shrieking Frieda tells him again that she will still love him, at which point he reveals yet another body part lost on the battlefield. Just as Frieda is telling him she will still love him in spite of his right foot having been amputated after becoming gangrenous in a mantrap, the drunk takes a turning and the words become indistinct. Everybody who has heard him knows the song, and how it finishes: the soldier continues to break news to Frieda about further losses of body parts until there is almost nothing left for her to love, and she tells him that she will still be his, no matter what. It is a simple song of true love – perhaps that is why it has remained so popular and why, even when sung by a drunk late at night, no reports are made of his antisocial behaviour.

The moth, huddling in the darkness, knows it to be a lie. But it is too late for anger. *Let them believe that if they want to. After all, they are only taking comfort, and who can blame them? For me, though, it is too late for comfort.* The voice fades, and fades, and soon it is gone altogether.

At ten past three the old man jolts awake at the sharp smack of wood on wood from one of the rooms below.

He sits up and listens for any further disturbance, but none occurs. He sets his alarm for five, then lies back and closes his eyes. He knows the sound, and that it can be dealt with later on. His mouth falls open, and once again his breathing fills the room, beginning as a light wheeze then escalating into a rattle, the inhalations and exhalations at a pitch so indistinguishable that it seems like a single undulating drone.

A fat house spider crawls across the sheet, clear against the bright white. It steps onto the sleeve of his nightshirt, where it lingers for a while before scuttling up to his neck. The moment the first of the eight dark brown legs touches the old man's cold skin he wakes once again. He does not move, but the rattle stops dead and his breathing becomes soft and shallow. The spider sprints to his cheek, where it remains still for a moment before moving towards his open mouth. It stops again, as if considering its next move, and then, with an agility bordering on grace, it darts into the chasm.

The old man's mouth shuts and the spider races around, trying to make its way out, but there is no escape from the thin, grey tongue that pushes it first into his cheek and then between his back teeth. After some final desperate flailing, the spider is crunched into a gritty paste and the tongue moves around the old man's teeth, collecting stray pieces.

His breathing slows, and he swallows the final traces. Soon the rattle returns. In and out, in and out. It all sounds the same.

II

At five o'clock the room filled with a furious beep. The old man extended a thin, grey arm and slid the alarm clock's switch to *off*. He rose to his feet, picked up a plastic torch and walked downstairs to find the source of the noise that had woken him in the night. It had come from one of the usual places, Room Eight, a small exhibition space at the back of the building. A flash of light showed him all he needed to see, and he went down to the desk by the main entrance. He picked up the telephone, and dialled.

'Yes?' came a man's voice after two rings, sprightly for so early in the morning.

'This is the museum.'

'Oh dear,' said the voice. 'Not bad news, I hope?'

'Yes. Bad news.'

'How awful.' There was a sigh. 'Could you tell me,

purely for medical reasons, if the prospective patient is male or female?'

'Female.'

'The poor lady.' He sighed again. 'I shall arrive at your back door in thirteen minutes.'

The old man used these thirteen minutes to return to his rooms and change from his nightshirt and nightcap into pressed black trousers, a black jacket, a brilliant white shirt and a black tie. His shoes shone a perfect black. He wore the same outfit every day, and he would often be mistaken for an undertaker. He almost never left the building, but when he did he found he was treated with misdirected deference, which suited him because nobody ever knew quite what to say, and he was able to avoid the vapid conversation that he found such a distasteful part of everyday life.

He stood beside the fire exit door to the rear of the building. There had never been a fire, and apart from the occasional delivery of a bulky exhibit it was used only for these visits from the doctor. The old man followed the seconds on his watch, and the knock came precisely on time. He opened the door and the doctor entered, his profession signalled by the black portmanteau in his hand and the stethoscope around his neck. He looked healthy, and his hair was thick for a man in middle age, though the dark brown was flecked with strands of white. He gave his usual sympathetic smile.

'I fear, Herr Schmidt,' he said, 'that once again we are too late.'

They walked upstairs to the scene of the incident. At the doorway the old man switched on the light and stood aside for the doctor to pass before following him in. A chair, the source of the noise that had woken him, had been kicked aside and lay upended on the floor. The woman's body hung absolutely still, her feet several inches above the floorboards. The pipe to which she had attached the rope remained in place.

'Oh dear,' sighed the doctor, his voice low as he assessed the familiar sight. 'Still,' he said, a trace of lightness returning to his tone, 'what's done is done. Let us begin.'

The old man left the room, and returned with a step-ladder. Quite used to the procedure, neither of them felt the need to speak. The doctor reached into his portmanteau for a folding serrated knife, which he handed to the old man, the taller of the two, who stepped up and started sawing through the rope at the point where the knot met the pipe. As fibres snowed down, the doctor delivered his post mortem.

'Interesting,' he said. 'Slow strangulation. Evidently she did not allow herself an adequate drop.' He picked up the chair she had kicked away, and nodded as his hypothesis was confirmed: her heels were not much lower than the seat. 'Just as I thought,' he said. 'She should have jumped from that table.' He pointed. 'It's higher.'

The woman's head was level with his. He took it in his hands and moved it from side to side. 'The neck doesn't appear to be broken,' he said, 'and judging by these fingernail marks on the throat it would seem that the unfortunate lady remained conscious for some time, trying quite desperately to save herself.' The old man stopped sawing for a moment to look at the scratches. He looked at her hands too. Her fingers were streaked with dry blood, and marked with burns from the rope. The doctor carried on. 'She would have fought for some time, maybe for as long as half an hour, realising all the time the terrible mistake she had made.' He sighed. 'What a shame that nobody heard a thing, that this poor creature could not have been rescued from her wrong turning.'

Neither of them had known this to happen before: whenever a visitor had chosen this manner of exit the doctor had found no evidence of a struggle. The well-executed incidents had resulted in a broken neck and instant death, and the less well-planned ones, with their insufficient drops or incorrectly positioned nooses, had apparently caused the person to black out as they fell, and they would hang, insensible, until the end.

His post mortem complete, the doctor stood aside as the final strands gave way and the body thumped to the floor. He removed the noose from the woman's neck, and pushed her tongue back into her mouth. 'Let's be absolutely sure,' he said, and listened for a while with his stethoscope before shaking his head.

They stood together, looking down at her. She had been around thirty, and was dressed in jeans and a thin, green jacket. The old man had seen her arrive, but he had not seen her leave. He paid as little attention as possible to the museum's visitors, but he had noticed a hunted look about her eyes, and had not been surprised to see her again. He said nothing.

'We must do this quickly,' said the doctor. 'After all, I am a busy general practitioner and I have not yet eaten my breakfast and, as any doctor will tell you, breakfast is the most important meal of the day.'

The old man felt no need to say anything, and assumed his established role in the removal of the body, leaning over to grab it by the wrists. The doctor lifted the ankles, and they made their way down to the back door. When they got there the doctor dropped his end, pushed the bar and peered into the alley. There was nobody around, so he darted out and opened the rear door of his large saloon car, which he had backed up close to the building. He raced back inside. 'Now,' he whispered. Together they hauled the body into the car. The doctor slammed it shut, and hurried round to the driver's seat. Without a word he got in and drove away.

The old man pulled the fire exit door closed and made his way up to Room Eight. He put the steps back in their cupboard, and the chair in its place in the corner, checking it for damage as he did. None was noticeable. He pulled a handkerchief from his pocket and wiped the seat. Very occasionally he would sit there, and he didn't want any muck from the woman's shoes ending up on his trousers.

Crouching, his knees stiff, he used his hands to wipe the sawn fibres into a pile, and wrapped them in the handkerchief. He picked up both lengths of rope, and had a final look around. He noticed her handbag was on the floor behind the display board. He picked it up, then went upstairs and dropped the pieces of rope into the kitchen bin. It had all been quite straightforward; he and the doctor had known these incidents to be a lot messier than this one. The cuffs of his brilliant white shirt remained spotless as he measured a fresh length from the coil of rope he kept under the sink, cut it, and tied an immaculate noose to replace the one the woman had taken from the display in the *Popular Methods* room. He wondered how long it would be before he was to find himself cutting yet another length of rope. A moment later he stopped wondering. It meant so little to him. It would happen when it happened.

III

It took little time for the doctor to drive from the city centre to the suburbs. As the old man was putting the newly tied noose in its place, he arrived back at his home, a detached house in a quiet, green neighbourhood. His gates and the door to his double garage opened automatically, and when they had clicked shut behind him he walked to the back of the car, opened it, looked down and sighed.

'You poor girl,' he whispered, as though she were sleeping and he must take care not to wake her. 'You poor girl.' He shook his head. 'Coffee first.' He opened the door to the kitchen, and went through.

Doctor Ernst Fröhlicher had moved to the city ten years earlier, bringing with him a black Labrador called Hans and a heart-stopping tale of tragedy. While looking for a house to settle in he had rented a room, and a short conversation with his landlady ensured that before his trunks were unpacked his story had spread through the streets around his practice. This was the extent of what was known: *Doctor Fröhlicher had married at the age of twenty-five, and been widowed at the age of twenty-eight.*

Noticing his wedding ring, his landlady had asked whether he would be joined at any point by Frau Fröhlicher, and on hearing his reply she had not found it possible to ask him to go on. The story remained unembellished as it passed from house to house, and everyone who heard it felt their heart turn to lead with pity. Barring only the smallest details they saw the same image in their minds, of a wife so beautiful and so gentle that to behold her would make the heart overflow with joy, and of a man quite superhuman in his courage as he faced the world alone, smiling as he devoted himself to healing others even though he was unable to mend his own broken heart. When, a few years into his time in the town, the doctor let slip to a talkative patient that his wife had died as a result of complications from a pregnancy, his heroic status soared to even further heights, and thus he was able to live alone as he entered middle age without a single eyebrow being raised, or so much as a whisper of innuendo passing from house to house.

His wife, Ute, had indeed been extraordinarily

beautiful, but his new neighbours were not to know that she had also been wayward, devious, scheming and, when it suited her, shrill. Nor were they to know that there had been a coldness to her beauty, her lips always on the verge of turning thin and her blue eyes quick to narrow into slits. Her mother had not been blind to her daughter's ways, and had often found herself suggesting that she stop all her nonsense, find a promising young professional and settle down. One day the girl surprised her by seeming to do just that.

The conventionally good-looking son of a nearby family was in the final stages of studying medicine, and hearing he was back for a few days, Ute had feigned a dizzy spell and requested a visit from him. The consultation took place in her bedroom, and the moment he walked in she let her white silk robe fall to the floor.

'I'm ready for my examination,' she said.

As his eyes took in the most wonderful sight he had ever seen, he had no idea what to do.

She helped him. 'Why not start here?' she said, taking one of his hands, guiding it downwards and gently pressing his middle finger to her, applying just the right amount of pressure as she guided it in a circular motion. He closed his eyes, and could feel the brush of the coarse, dark hairs, and the warmth, and the moisture. 'I'm feeling dizzy again,' she whispered, 'but in a different way from before.' She let out a series of small, breathy yelps, and touched his cheek with a single finger. 'A very different way.'

She moved his hand to one of her breasts, making sure the soft golden hair she had shaken loose brushed against his fingers. 'Have you found the root of the problem yet?' she asked, her mouth open just a little as she moved closer to him. She took his spare hand, and guided it to her other breast. 'Do you think it could be glandular?' As she pushed her body into his she could feel that she had conquered him.

'Oh, doctor,' she said.

'Well, I am not yet qualified, and I suggest you . . .' Her lips brushed against his, and at last the world made sense. Everything he had strived for and everything he had lived through had been a stepping-stone leading him to this: the moment he found out what it meant to love somebody with every cell in his body. He had always had a sense that he had been looking for something, and he had found it right there in the soft lips that no longer brushed against his but devoured them, and in the smooth back that undulated beneath the touch of his fingers, and when they finally disengaged from their kiss it was there in the face that looked up at him, a face so immaculate that for a moment he thought nature unkind for not having made all women as perfect as the one in his arms.

Her fingers moved down to his belt buckle, and three months later her mother stood in church and looked on as her nineteen-year-old daughter exchanged vows with this handsome and promising young professional.

She wanted to be happy for them, but no matter how hard she tried, it wasn't possible. She had only ever seen her child look so demure when she had been up to something, and the joy and relief she should have felt was eclipsed by worry for her new son-in-law, and a creeping sense of guilt for having wished this terrible fate upon him.

Ute's mother's fears had not been misplaced. As the honeymooners paddled at sunset in the Mediterranean Sea, the bride told her husband that she had only married him to get back at her much older lover for refusing to leave his wife. She called a passing stranger, handed over their camera and asked for a photograph. 'Look happy,' she whispered. 'I'll make sure he gets a copy. It'll drive him insane.'

The young man felt as if he had been punched in the belly as he placed his arm around his bride's shoulders, and smiled.

'Don't worry though,' she said, when the stranger had handed back the camera, 'I'll still let you fuck me.'

To his horror, he found his heart gladdened by these words.

As they set up home together, Ute complained about the modest size of their apartment, railed at the time he devoted to his junior position at the hospital when he could have been dancing attendance on her, and did little to hide her readiness to yield to temptation in his absence. The onslaught never abated. Even on her death bed, when she had known there was no chance of recovery, she had refused to say she was sorry for the way she had treated him, and she used the last of her energy to imply that the baby, by this time lost, had almost certainly been her lover's, the one she had gone so far out of her way to spite. 'Now he'll be sorry,' she said, her beauty more powerful than ever as it shone from her ashen face. The doctor still loved her completely, and even though he felt a sense of release when this awful child's heart stopped beating, it was a release he would never have wished for.

The people who heard his story were right when they shook their heads and supposed that nobody would ever be able to take her place.

The doctor tickled Hans behind his ears, and while the coffee was percolating he found his camera, returned to the garage and opened the back of the car. He took some photographs then braced himself, picked up the body and carried it to one of his four large chest freezers. Smiling, he heaved it in, closed the lid and went back inside. There was still time for breakfast before Hans' walk.

He opened the refrigerator and pulled out a thick slice of meat, which he fried in dripping and seasoned with a sprinkling of salt and pepper. When it was ready he put it on a plate and ate it, throwing the occasional piece to the grateful dog. 'This will set me up amply for the morning ahead,' he said, 'and for the sake of balance I shall eat an apple as we walk in the park. After all, Hans, it is important to receive a range of nutrients, particularly at breakfast time, and folk wisdom and modern science are united in telling us that there are few foods more nutritious than the apple.'

Hans had heard these sounds many times before.

The doctor scraped the bone into the bin and put the plate in the dishwasher. 'Come, Hans,' he said. The dog bounded for the front door and waited to be put on his lead.

IV

After putting the noose in its place the old man spent some time sitting at his kitchen table, where he ate a single cracker and drank a glass of water. His breakfast over, he sat and looked straight ahead, glancing every once in a while at the clock on the wall as he waited for the time his duties would begin.

At eight fifty-eight he stood and made his way downstairs. On the stroke of nine he opened the front door to see the large, smiling face of a powerfully built young woman, her light brown hair sitting in a chaotic pile on top of her head. Her name was Hulda. It was the correct name for her. Every once in a while a Hulda will come along who is able to pass through life discreetly, but most of them are so thoroughly *Hulda* that there is no other name they could possibly have been given. Shopkeepers, ticket inspectors and tourists in search of directions will greet them with the words, *Good morning, Hulda*, or, *Excuse me, Hulda*. This happens so naturally, and with such frequency, that neither party stops to think it strange.

'What a lovely day,' she said. 'Cooler than yesterday, but still almost cloudless. And I brought this,' she chuckled, as she held up her umbrella, 'just in case. I always seem to expect the worst. I suppose it must be a habit I picked up in my mid-to-late childhood, when everything was so difficult for me.'

He said nothing as she walked past him. He bolted the door then sat at the front desk, where he sorted through a small pile of mail. A minute later he looked up to see she had emerged from the cupboard under the stairs. With her mop, bucket and broom lined up and ready to go she stood before him, whistling as she snapped on a pair of rubber gloves.

'Do you know that tune?' she asked.

The old man had heard it before, as it played on other people's radios. He said nothing.

'It's called "Live is Life". It's by an Austrian rock group called Opus, and is all about how much they enjoy playing concerts.'

He continued to say nothing.

'It's quite a silly song, but I like it because it reminds me of my childhood.'

He wondered how anybody could enjoy being reminded of their childhood.

'Or at least my childhood up until the age of eight.

I was born the year it became a hit, you see, and my elder sister, who was a teenager at the time, bought me a copy as a gift. When I was just two days old she stood outside one of their concerts and waited for them to sign it just for me. There were many fans there, and she could only get the autograph of their drummer, Günter Grasmuck. She told me as I lay in my crib that she thought he was the most handsome man she had ever seen, and that one day she was going to marry him. And do you know what?'

He clenched and unclenched his long, grey fingers as Hulda carried on.

'Four years ago, in a quiet civil ceremony in the small Austrian city of Eisenstadt, my sister became the fifth, and we can only hope final, Frau Günter Grasmuck.' The old man stood and started walking up the stairs, but Hulda carried on. 'I'm only joking, Herr Schmidt. My sister didn't really marry Günter Grasmuck. In truth she married a man called Günter Grünbaum, an under-floor heating specialist from Ulm. To clarify though, she *did* stand outside the concert to get Herr Grasmuck's autograph for me when I was just a baby, and although she had wanted to marry him, it turned out to be the only time they met.' The further the old man went up the stairs the louder her voice became. 'Every year on my birthday we would play the song and sing along, even when it had fallen out of fashion. Every year until I turned eight, because that was when my mother met the man who was to become my stepfather and things began to go wrong for both of us, but for me in particular.' He had gone from view, and she was now shouting at the top of her voice, her head tilted back and her hands cupped around her mouth. 'My sister had left home by that point and was unaware of our difficulties, and didn't feel the need to protect us.'

A door slammed upstairs, and Hulda smiled as she went through to Room Four, *Unfortunate Survivors*. She began by dusting the frame of a photograph of an American boy, half his face a mess of scar tissue. His parents had blamed heavy metal, but Hulda had a feeling there was more to the story than that. Whenever she looked at him she hoped his life had improved since the picture had been taken.

'*Every minute of the future*,' she sang, '*is a memory of the past.*'

At ten twenty-nine they stood in the hallway, by the bolted front door. Hulda smiled at her superior. She saw him as somebody who needed to be brought out of himself, and had long ago decided that she would be the one to do the bringing out. 'We're quite a team aren't we, Herr Schmidt?' she said.

He looked at his watch. At precisely ten thirty he unbolted the door, and with a bright smile and a *See you tomorrow*, Hulda went away. He hooked the door open, walked over to his desk and waited for people to arrive, hoping nobody would. But they did. His first visitors, a young man and a young woman, came in just before eleven o'clock. Lovers or siblings, he couldn't tell. Maybe they were both. It was nothing to him. They wore matching waterproof jackets and carried identical backpacks. They didn't look towards him as they passed, and they left after fifteen minutes, just long enough for them to have gone from room to room without stopping to look closely at anything. They put no money in the donation box, and before they were out of the door they were already huddling over a map, looking for the next attraction to visit. A few mumbled words about when and where they were planning to eat lunch told him they were from northern Italy, somewhere between Milan and Verona, most likely Travagliato or Gussago. He had heard this accent spoken before, and felt no satisfaction in hearing it again.

One thirty, the time allotted for the guided tour, passed with no takers, as it had done every day since the museum opened. The old man left his post to go to the lavatory. When he returned to his desk he found an unmarked envelope lying there. He sat down and eyed it for a moment before sliding it towards himself with a long, grey finger. Inside was a handwritten note. It was unsigned, and just a few sentences long. He thought its confessional hysteria ludicrous, but for a moment he almost smiled. *Pavarotti's wife will love this*, he thought. He slipped it into the inside pocket of his jacket.

* * *

At five o'clock he closed the front door. The day had ended with a total of twenty-six visitors, not one of whom had stayed for any length of time or made an enquiry. He emptied the donation box and found two euros thirty, which he entered in the logbook. Then in the *Visitor Numbers* column he wrote *78*. He had worked in museums for some years, and had always found it helpful to treble the real figures whenever possible.

Switching off lights as he went, he made his way back to his rooms, where he ate a chunk of bread and a slice of hardening cheese, ironed a brilliant white shirt for the morning and started rereading the Þ section of an Icelandic–German dictionary. It was all very familiar, and around *Þjónari, Þjónkan* and *Þjónn*, his eyelids began to fall. He got up and changed into his nightshirt and nightcap, then remembered the woman's bag. He emptied its contents on to the kitchen table. There was a small mirror, some tampons, a paperback novel, an unopened packet of chewing gum, a ballpoint pen, a small tin of lip balm, some old train, bus and cinema tickets, and a wallet which he opened to find a credit card, and a driving licence that told him her name and that she had lived in Frankfurt. From the photograph he could see she had looked much the same in life as she had in death. A zipped compartment revealed the only item he was interested in keeping: a twenty-Euro note. Everything else went into the bin.

With no reason to stay awake any longer, he lay on his narrow bed and pulled the white sheet over his body. He looked into the darkness. The street was quiet, and no noises came from the rooms below. His eyes closed and his mouth opened. No spider crawled in.

V

The old man rose at six. In bare feet, and still in his nightshirt and nightcap, he began his weekly rounds, making sure there was nothing that would surprise the museum's proprietor and her husband on their visit. Following the suggested route, he started in Room One, *Through The Ages*, where he checked the exhibits for damage. The sculpture of Antony and Cleopatra was fine, and so were the portraits of Heinrich von Kleist and Vincent van Gogh, and the holographic representation of the self-immolation of Thích Quảng Đúc. He walked through to Room Two, *Reasons Why*. Once again nothing had been disturbed, and Hulda's cleaning had been thorough.

It was not long before he reached Room Eleven, *Familiar Faces*, which was situated in the basement and marked the end of the suggested route. On the half-landing hung a large painting of a young Billy Joel, his face contorted in despair as he drank from a bottle of furniture polish. Pavarotti's wife had read about the singer's anguish and of his unusual choice of self-administered poison, and when she heard he was coming to the city to play a concert in the castle grounds she had immediately commissioned an artist's impression of the scene and written a long letter inviting the subject to unveil it. To her mystification he had not responded, and the painting had ended up being hung without fanfare. The old man paid it the minimum of attention as he continued down the stairs and through the doors.

Room Eleven was the largest of the exhibition spaces. It began with two photographs of Marilyn Monroe: in the first she was subduing her billowing skirt in a promotional still for *The Seven Year Itch*, and in the second she was lying in the morgue, her beauty gone so completely that it was as if it had only ever been a mirage, or a trick. Then came a photograph of Kurt Cobain's right leg, a charcoal drawing of Ernest Hemingway, a knitted doll of the Singing Nun, a scale model of the Hollywood sign complete with a four-inch Peg Entwistle plummeting from the top of the letter H, and a dolls' house with the walls cut away to reveal Sylvia Plath with her head in a gas oven, her children asleep in the next room. Next there was an exceptionally lifelike waxwork of Yukio Mishima in his final moments, his face impassive as he held a sword in his hand, his guts spilling from a slit across his belly. This was the museum's most photographed exhibit, with tourists taking turns to stand beside it with their thumbs aloft, as if this was Madame Tussaud's and he was Indiana Jones or Enrique Iglesias. Beside Mishima was an embedded television screen. The old man pushed a button and a minute-long silent film began, showing a re-creation of Virginia Woolf's fateful wade into the River Ouse, her pockets filled with stones. Without interest he watched it to the end, then moved on to the small but life-size dummies of Hervé Villechaize and David Rappaport, each in their own diorama – Villechaize slumped beside a patio door and Rappaport lying under a bush and being discovered, too late, by curious dogs. This side of the room finished with a card-board cut-out of a leather-trousered Michael Hutchence, and as the old man passed it he was not surprised to see that on the singer's hand, the one holding the micro-phone, somebody had written the words *WANKING ACCIDENT*. This happened from time to time, and the old man carried the cut-out to the store cupboard and piled it up with all the others that had been defaced by visitors who felt this exhibit had no place in the museum. He was irritated by the thought that at some point he would have to go to the trouble of throwing them away. There were only four clean spares left, and as he took one of them out of the cupboard he knew it would not be long before it too was to join the pile of rejects. He made a mental note to order yet another batch.

When the fresh cut-out was in place, the old man moved on to the other side of the room, where the theme lightened. First came Brigitte Bardot, then Gary Coleman, Owen Wilson, Elizabeth Taylor, Halle Berry, Sinéad O'Connor, Vanilla Ice, Tina Turner and Tuesday Weld. It was no accident that these were the last exhibits on the suggested route. They were all photographs taken after their failures, the subjects looking straight into the camera and smiling – smiles which, as Pavarotti's wife had emphasised time and again, they would never have smiled had their plans not gone awry. She called them *smiles of inspiration*. To her the museum was a prevention initiative, a way of dissuading people whose thoughts might be heading in the wrong direction, of confronting them with the reality of taking such a step. These photographs, she frequently explained, were there to remind their visitors that there is always hope, that they must hold on through the bad times.

The old man felt his usual small surge of distaste at the sight of these faces, then returned to his apartment in the eaves, where he sat at the kitchen table, took a single cracker from a tin and put it in his mouth. He chewed for a while, staring straight ahead as his thin, grey tongue darted around his mouth, picking pieces from the gaps between his teeth.

'Another pleasant morning,' said Hulda at precisely nine o'clock, 'although this could change later on.

Who would be a meteorologist? Certainly not me. And not you either. No, you have chosen instead to go into the world of museums, and what an interesting world it is too.' The one-woman cacophony continued as she walked inside and went to her cupboard. By the time she emerged, he was halfway up the stairs. 'Are you looking forward to your weekly meeting?' she called. He didn't respond. She smiled to herself. As always on these days she would spend her ninety minutes checking that the entrance shone brightly, inside and out. She wanted to make sure she wasn't in a far-flung room when Pavarotti arrived. Something about him made her feel light-headed, and she couldn't stop herself from wishing that theirs was not a professional relationship, and that she could ask him if he had a brother, a brother who was like him in every way but who might be unlucky in love and still searching for the right girl. A sturdy girl, perhaps, who has been through difficult times but emerged a stronger person, always eager to see the sunny side of any situation.

She opened the front door, stepped outside and breathed a light mist on to the brass plate, which she rubbed with her cloth. When she stepped back to inspect her work, her smiling face was reflected in the metal. She looked at the blue sky. At times like this it almost seemed as if she wasn't going to Hell. She knew she was though, and there was nothing she could do about it. In the meantime there was plenty to be getting on with, starting with mopping the tiles in the entrance hall.

At nine thirty the old man walked down the stairs to see Hulda greeting Pavarotti and his wife as enthusiastically as propriety would allow. He extended his hand to meet theirs, his fingers cold and dry in their fleshy grips. Hulda watched them go up to their meeting.

By the time they reached the old man's kitchen, Pavarotti was out of breath. Sweat had dripped into his thick black beard, and he dabbed his face with a handkerchief, which changed in moments from sky blue to navy. He noticed the old man's eyes upon him. 'It has been something of a busy morning,' he said in his defence. His voice was thin and high, and seemed not to belong to him; it was nothing like the dramatic rumble that might be expected from a man of his appearance.

They sat around the table. 'To business, gentlemen?' said his wife. She was short, and shaped like Queen Victoria, her silver hair tied into a bun and her face grave.

Pavarotti poised his pen, ready to take the minutes, and the old man gave the faintest of nods as he wondered when she was going to produce the cake.

Every week, at some apparently random point of the meeting, Pavarotti's wife would present him with a large home-made chocolate cake. He had difficulty

concentrating on her opening topic, *Strategies for facili-
tating an increase in visitor numbers*, partly because the
few visitors the museum already received were enough
of a nuisance to him, but also because he could think
of little besides the cake. For now, though, it remained
concealed inside her large bag.

These meetings were usually little more than
monologues, with the old man giving the occasional
nod and Pavarotti keeping his eyes lowered as he
transcribed everything his wife said. In spite of his
size, Pavarotti always remained in his wife's shadow,
and the old man knew very little about him. He had
learned that he ran a small chain of candle shops, and
that with his wife he was father to four daughters –
Liesl, Chloris, Dagmar and Swanhilde. There was
plenty he did not know. He didn't know, for example,
that it was only at these meetings when Pavarotti's
voice became so high and so thin, that when he was
at home with his children, and at work among the
candles, it had a depth to it, and an authority. The old
man also had no idea that Pavarotti was just twenty-
six years old.

Pavarotti's wife had been born into a family that lived
for opera. Her mother and father had hoped their child
would be just as intoxicated by it as they were, and
they were not disappointed. She was happy to spend
her weekends and school holidays accompanying them
on trips to the major houses of the world to watch the

classics, and to festivals to hear revivals of obscure pieces, and on school nights she would often sit in on rehearsals of productions by the local company, of which her parents were enthusiastic patrons.

When she was seven years old she was taken to La Scala, where she saw a rising star called Luciano Pavarotti singing the part of Tebaldo in Bellini's *I Capuleti e i Montecchi*. She knew from the moment he stepped on stage that he was as desirable as it was possible for a man to be. Looking down from her box she found herself overwhelmed by his beard, his black hair, his twinkling eyes and his magnificent shape. He didn't appear to be fat, nor even overweight, he just looked powerful, and when he opened his mouth to sing this power was confirmed beyond doubt. The experience rendered her mute for an entire fortnight. Her parents were not at all concerned, having them-selves been struck dumb by the opera for long periods of time, and they calmly brought her soup and fruit while they waited for her to snap back to life. As she lay in bed for those two weeks, staring at the ceiling and reliving every moment of the concert, she began to accept that a union with the singer was out of the question. She was just a seven-year-old girl, awkward and bashful, and even though she would soon be eight and would one day be a woman, she understood that the thick shape of her body and the coarse texture of her hair could never bring him the joy she felt he deserved. Such a man would consort only with angels.

She let him go then, and once she had said goodbye to her dream she went down to breakfast. As she sat with her parents, she put down her grapefruit spoon and spoke. 'Mother, Father,' she said, 'I very much enjoyed our visit to La Scala. I thought the young tenor Pavarotti quite exceptional.'

They smiled because they too had very much enjoyed their visit, and thought Pavarotti quite exceptional.

As the singer's fame grew she could feel him drifting even farther from her reach, but she clung to the hope of meeting somebody who could be her own Pavarotti – not the celestial creature she had seen on the stage but a Pavarotti in human form, with perhaps just one or two of his epic qualities. On reaching the age of forty-one she finally gave up hope, and accepted that there was nothing she could do but continue to devote herself to a productive spinsterhood. Then one night, at a charity gala that she had helped to organise, she saw a young man standing alone on the other side of the hall. For a moment her heart stopped, then she swept over and introduced herself. She found that he was there not to socialise but to hear one of his favourite soloists singing one of his favourite pieces, and on being told that she had booked the soloist and chosen the piece, he complimented her taste. The performance was about to begin and she was obliged to return to her duties, but not before inviting him to dinner so they could continue their conversation.

Two days later they met again, and before they had

reached the end of the main course she broke off from their discussion of the strengths and shortcomings of Salieri's *Axur, Re d'Ormus* to say, 'You do realise, don't you, that time is against us? We must start trying for children at the earliest opportunity. I mean, of course, within the realm of decency.' The boy raised no objections, because by this time he had fallen quite in love with her. The conversation immediately returned to a light-hearted comparison of Lorenzo da Ponte's libretto with that of Pierre Beaumarchais, and he continued to nod his assent as she offered to pile extra helpings of food on his plate. As they said goodnight she lifted her face and he kissed her. It was the first time for both of them, and they proceeded the only way they knew, with a passion that was truly operatic.

'You will grow a beard for me?' she asked, breathless, when this kiss at last came to an end.

He nodded, and headed into the night, his belly almost ready to burst.

Six weeks later they married, and by then he had gained so much weight that he had to have a new cummerbund fitted at the last minute. Within a year Liesl had arrived in the world to the sound of Wagner's *Tannhäuser*, a sterilised pianist playing in the corner of the room as the teenage father took the part of Wolfram and his wife, sweating and pushing, sang Elisabeth. By this time his beard had grown quite substantially, not quite to the density it would later reach, but already thick and black against his boyish complexion. His hair had grown too, and he wore it swept back from his substantial brow. The likeness she had spotted at the gala, then little more than a suggestion, was reaching a level beyond which she had ever wished for, but she was relieved and delighted to find it was not only this resemblance that she loved. She also loved the way he looked at her as if she was the only woman in the world, the way he pursued his dream of running a small chain of candle shops without once asking her for financial support, the way conversation and song flowed so freely between them, and how, whenever he came in from work with the twinkle in his eye that had resulted in Liesl, Chloris, Dagmar and Swanhilde, her body fizzed with pleasure, readying itself to melt into his.

They had not assumed that children would come, and had never dared to hope for four in such quick succession. She often felt her heart leap with joy at the thought of this family that had almost never been. Before long though, this elation would pass, leaving only pity for those who had not found such happiness. As she settled into her marriage she thought about such people more and more. She worried that with the absence of contentment from their lives they might sink into despair and start thinking terrible thoughts. She had known the relentless nag of sadness, and there had been times when it had seemed it would never end, times when she had almost lost her strength of character, but she had always found within her the will to pick herself up and carry on. She could never stop herself from worrying about those who lacked her fortitude, and she was overcome with an urgent need to save these people from themselves. When she inherited a large house in the old part of the city she knew immediately what she would do with it. Six months later the brass plate was screwed into the wall, and the museum opened its doors to the public.

She finished outlining her strategies for increasing visitor numbers, and the old man was satisfied that he would be able to find ways of keeping them all from being implemented. He had become adept at quashing her ideas while making it appear as if he was regretful that they could not, for some practical reason, reach fruition. He would cite prohibitive expense, health and safety implications, or another museum having beaten them to the idea. These reasons were often fabricated; he would do whatever it took to keep his days free of upheaval. Pavarotti's wife had no idea that a war was going on, a war she was losing on many fronts. Sometimes, though, one of her ideas would get through his wall of resistance and a small change would be made, usually a new exhibit or a minor alteration of layout, and the old man would, in this small defeat, be strategically cooperative, even helpful.

Her opening subject over, Pavarotti's wife changed tack and started talking in a low voice about a recent trip to the dentist with Dagmar, who had been suffering from an excruciating toothache. It was a mundane anecdote, but the experience had reminded her of the very reason for the museum's existence. The sight of her child in pain, and the helplessness she had felt at her own inability to comfort her, had awoken the misery and dread that lurks in the heart of every parent. Uninvited thoughts barged into her mind and wouldn't leave; wild imaginings loomed before her as though they were real and urgent threats. These feelings were never far away. Sometimes, as with the toothache, there would be a catalyst, but often these worries jumped out of nowhere. While watering her house plants she would see an image of Liesl being flattened by a falling girder, or of Chloris, an enthusiastic needle worker even at her young age, entangling herself in a ball of cotton yarn and slowly, irrevocably, turning blue. Sometimes as she polished the silverware she would picture Dagmar having a happy and carefree childhood, but in her late teens falling in love with a dashing Finn who could never return this love and, thinking it the kindest way, telling her so, and the girl becoming so unhappy that this child who had been so full of life and joy, no longer wished to stay alive. And then there were the times when she saw Swanhilde developing a mental difficulty that came from within and which was far beyond her control or anybody else's, a difficulty that engulfed her, and made her prone to the darkest thoughts, thoughts upon which, in a moment of terror, a moment in which there was nobody there to help her, she might act.

43

The girder would be a dreadful accident, the ball of yarn a random tragedy: it was the last two that assaulted Pavarotti's wife with the most force. It was thoughts such as these, and the possibility that one of her children, or indeed anybody's child, would end up this way that had driven her to open the museum. But she said none of this, she just continued the story of her trip to the dentist, describing in great detail the extraction of the tooth. She didn't mention that Dagmar's every wail had been a brutal reminder of her child's mortality, and that of all her daughters.

The meeting was nearing its end, and the old man was invited to give his usual summary of the week. He included his doctored visitor numbers, and made no mention of having found a body in Room Eight the day before. When this was done, he reached into his breast pocket. 'This arrived yesterday,' he said. He handed the letter to Pavarotti's wife, who put on her reading glasses and looked it over.

'But this is wonderful,' she said, almost breathless. She carried on reading to the end. 'It is just this kind of correspondence that reminds us that our venture is so worthwhile.' She stood and read it aloud, her voice rising and falling as though she were on stage:

> Friends, I came to your museum a man with a heart laden with the burden of darkness, looking for hints and tips for taking the easy way out. But I now realise that this is not the

purpose of your estimable establishment. Nothing struck me more than the futility of joining what you so rightly describe as 'this heartrending cascade of human lemmings'. I know it will not be easy, that there will be times when I shall once again drink deep from my tankard of despair, but even so I now face the future with a renewed sense of purpose and, dare I say it, optimism. You are a beacon of light in the darkness. Thank you.

'*Your estimable establishment*,' she repeated. '*A beacon of light in the darkness*. Have there ever been higher compliments? Gentlemen, we have saved him.'

Her delight didn't last. She looked at the ceiling and said, quietly, 'But our work goes on. Every day we hear of unhappy souls who were not fortunate enough to have passed through our doors, and who are no longer here for us to save. This, gentlemen,' she looked from one to the other as she held up the letter, 'is why an increase in visitor numbers is so crucial. This afternoon I shall begin writing to the editors of publications around the world in the hope that our call will be heard. We must rescue as many such unfortunates as we can. If we can only get these people through our door then they will be saved, and get them through the door we must, no matter who they are or where they are from.' She spread her arms wide. 'We must reach out to every corner of the globe.'

* * *

Whenever the old man heard a visitor speak, he would more often than not know where they had come from, every nuance of their diction bringing forward a place name. For thirty years he had worked in a government linguistics department, doing little besides sitting in what was referred to as *the laboratory*, listening to recordings of speaking voices from around the world. Regardless of the language, as soon as he had heard an accent from a particular region its idiosyncrasies would be locked into his mind, the knowledge ready for retrieval at any moment. Every once in a while somebody would come into the laboratory and play him a bugged telephone conversation or a recording of a ransom demand. He would tell them where the speaker's accent indicated they came from, and the person with the recording would go away again. Usually he heard no more about it, but sometimes he would find himself being commended for his crucial role in an investigation. As populations became increasingly mobile he was able to peel apart the various layers of accent with considerable accuracy. He was largely indifferent to this talent, but even after so many years he still felt a light thud of satisfaction upon encountering an inflection or an intonation he had not previously heard outside the laboratory. A pin would go in the map that he carried in his mind.

To his disappointment, Pavarotti's wife's publicity drive will not be without success, but with the increase in visitors will come new voices, and every once in a while he will feel this light thud. It will happen on hearing the man from Mindanao, and the child from Opobo.

Before the year is out the old man will encounter a voice from Portugal, and he will know at once that it belongs to somebody who has grown up in a small town high in the hills some way to the north of the Rio Douro. The voice will be quiet, and devoid of even the faintest trace of hope, but this will not interest him; all that will matter is the map that flashes in his mind. Within moments any satisfaction will be gone, succeeded by a feeling of irritation at the thought of the inevitable inconvenience of the call to the doctor, and the clearing up, and a sense of impatience as he waits for them to get it over with.

But that is all to come, and for now his eyes widen as Pavarotti's wife reaches into her bag and pulls out a large silver tin.

VI

A little over twenty-one years earlier, on a cold January night in a small house in a small town in the Portuguese hills, some way to the north of the Rio Douro, a boy was born. When the midwife had gone away the new parents, alone at last, gazed at their first born as he lay sleeping in his crib. After a few minutes they both looked up, and each could tell from the other's expression that they had noticed the same thing, something which neither had expected. Saying nothing, they both wondered why the midwife had made no mention of it. She had seemed impatient to clear up and go as quickly as she could; maybe she knew that nothing she could say would make any difference, and this was something the parents needed to find out for themselves. They went back to looking at him, and tried to dismiss these thoughts. After all, it had been a long day and sometimes the mind plays tricks, but no matter how long or how hard they looked it was always there. They thought back to long conversations in which they had agreed that they would love their child just the same no matter what, and they told themselves that this was the case, that nothing in the world would have made them love him any more or any less. He blinked open his eyes, and seemed for a moment to be looking straight at them, from one to the other. At last they spoke.

'Oh,' said the mother.

'I know,' said the father, and he reached into the crib and scooped him up, this little thing that had opened chambers of his heart that he had never known were there.

In the days that followed, people from the town came to visit the boy, who had been named Mauro. As is customary the men stood at the back of the room, blankly nodding their approval as the women got on with the business of leaning over the crib and offering exuberant compliments on the handsomeness of the child, telling the new parents that one day he would be breaking hearts. As they delivered these well-worn speeches they began to feel uneasy, wondering whether it was right for them to be saying such things about this boy. Even the men, who on these occasions would usually notice almost nothing about the baby as they drifted into daydreams, could see that this one was different. They had all been struck by the same quality that his parents had noticed that first night: as he lay there with a length that was sure to translate into height, a head of thick, black hair, flawless skin, and features already well-defined, the women found that for the first time in their life they truly meant the words they were saying, that he really *was* handsome, and that he really *would* break hearts. Whenever he opened his eyes they shone with an irresistible sparkle. Nobody had ever seen anything quite like it, and the visitors began to wonder whether such an incredible boy would ever find a match in this small town.

It didn't take long for the answer to arrive.

When the boy was a few weeks old, just as it seemed as if the winter was never going to end, another child was born, this time a girl. At the onset of her mother's labour an icy wind had been blowing through the town, but by the time the baby came into the world the air was still and warm. Everybody who visited in the days that followed was only half joking when they said she had brought the springtime with her. As they looked at her, wriggling and wrapped in a simple blanket, they saw that her nose was delicate and her eyes large, seeming to smile as she looked up at them. Mauro and Madalena were by no means the only new arrivals in the town, but without exception the visitors' thoughts turned to the beautiful boy. Even the boy's own mother knew, the moment she saw the baby girl. She held her son over the crib and said, 'Look, Mauro. Look at Madalena.

Isn't she pretty? Maybe one day you'll marry her.' She would have said this anyway, but she found the words ringing true. The boy's father had been standing at the back of the room, and even from his oblique vantage point he could see this as well. Neither of them said a word about it; they both knew that there was nothing they could do but wait for the story to unfold.

The children began to steal glances at one another at school and in church, and soon afterwards they became playmates, racing through the fields and up into the mountains, at first with the other children and then, as they got older, dashing ahead or dawdling, just the two of them. At first neither really knew why they were drawn together, but this could never last. Words of warning were given and boundaries set, but one day there was a change between them, and from then on they found every opportunity to slip behind rocks and into gulleys, and one summer afternoon, when both were fourteen and the promise of their babyhoods had been confirmed beyond doubt, they were seen together in the town square, sitting in the shade of a tree in such a way that everybody knew that a vow of love had, at last, been exchanged.

As they glided through the streets and the fields they were almost as unreal as images on a billboard, and life for everybody else in the town was able to go on as normal. Just as the people of Rome continue to hang pictures on the walls of their apartments in spite of the proximity of the Sistine Chapel, so were Mauro and Madalena's neighbours able to look at their husbands, wives and sweethearts with as much fondness as if these two had not been breathing the same clean mountain air. The other young people formed romances among themselves, each knowing that the other was not technically the most attractive person in town, but never mentioning it and not letting it matter. Sometimes, though, an unfortunate youth would go through a phase of suffering pangs of longing for Madalena or for Mauro, but the pair bore their looks and their love graciously, and whenever one of them caught somebody gazing at them with yearning in their eyes they would smile back, a smile that gave no encouragement but was infused with a warm, benevolent pity. These smiles said, *I know why you're looking at me in that way, and I'm sorry, but don't despair. You'll find somebody right for you one day, I just know it.* The unhappy soul would understand this wordless exchange, and take comfort until they found they could at last get on with their lives. At least that was what would usually happen. Not everybody in town was able to shake off their yearning so easily though, and one pair of eyes was the saddest of all.

Every time Madalena saw these eyes they were blazing with a helpless love for her, and this love never faded with time, it only grew, flying at her as the boy gazed across the schoolyard. He left school to begin working at his family's bakery, and every time she walked past the shop, his love would power its way through the glass before landing, unwanted, in her heart.

The older generations noticed the young baker's predicament with dismay. *It's such a shame he won't be marrying any time soon*, they thought to themselves. *If only his heart hadn't taken him down a dead end.* From before he was born they had all been looking forward to his wedding day, but now it seemed they had been waiting in vain.

Of all the weddings in a small town, one in a baker's family is looked forward to more than any other. Guests leave the wedding of a butcher's child with bellies weighed down with meat, their evening blighted by the knowledge that it will keep them awake and take days to pass through their systems. The marriage of the mortician's daughter takes place under a cloud of darkness, the congregation seeing the young couple not as they are, but as they will be when the time to let go has finally passed and they lie, still and cold, in wooden boxes. The candlestick maker's celebration is plagued by constant annoyance as guests singe their arm hair as they reach for condiments, and wax drips on to dresses that had been made for the occasion from a fabric so delicate that they know it will be beyond restoration. The hosts, quite used to being around so many flames, will be unaware of the torment that surrounds them, and will deem the day a great success. A wedding in a baker's family, though, is a day of sweet tastes, and of pastry flakes that can be brushed to the floor with ease to be licked up by happy dogs. As the children of these families grow up there is a sense of impatience for them to marry so a wedding feast can be held. This pressure is never expressed, but it will be keenly felt, and this is at least partly why they have always married so young, and why the phrase *a baker's generation* is used in so many languages to denote a period of time slightly shorter than a conventional generation. The family of the sad-eyed boy was no different. For baker's generation after baker's generation they had married when they were not long out of school, but as he entered his late teens it was clear to everybody that the boy who loved Madalena so hopelessly was going to depart from the tradition.

The boy's father had married as expected. A baker's generation earlier he had barely begun shaving when the church bells had rung out for him and his bride. The whole town had turned out to wish them well, and the celebrations had gone on deep into the night, the couple glowing with the joy of it all. The only discordant note had come when the groom was taken to one side by his great-great-grandmother, who gripped his arm and said, in a voice at once firm and gentle, 'While you children are away on your honeymoon I shall take every opportunity to pray that your marriage will be a fruitful one. My prayer will, however, contain a simple caveat, namely that you do not conceive a child while you are there,' she pointed a bony finger diagonally downwards, 'in your hotel by the sea. When you return, that will be the time.'

He had not asked her to elaborate. He thanked her for her good wishes and her prayers, and went back to dance with his bride, to hold her in his arms and dream of what awaited them in their hotel by the sea.

Shortly after their return home, his wife began to have unusual pains in her belly. A trip to the doctor confirmed that a baby was on its way, and they rushed to tell their families, who met up after hours at the bakery and fell into an impromptu celebration. The festivities were interrupted by the great-great-grandmother of the father-to-be, who had been sitting alone in the corner and refusing all offers of food and wine. She stood up and banged her stick three times on the floor.

The room fell silent.

'This celebration is all very well,' she said, 'and of course we shall welcome the newcomer with all our hearts, but remember this: the child was conceived between the crisp cotton sheets of the honeymoon hotel.' The young couple blushed, and everybody waited for her to continue. 'This means,' she said, looking from blank face to blank face, 'that the baby is due to enter the world in early March.' A chill emanated from the aunts and uncles. While some of the women had already estimated the baby's due date, its significance had not struck them until this moment. The younger members of the party waited for the old woman to continue. 'If the child arrives when it is due, it will be born under the sign of the fish.' She drew the sign in the air with the end of her stick. 'This town has not seen a Piscean child for many decades, and the last one . . . Well, maybe it's time you young people were told about him.'

The older relatives implored her not to tell. 'Please,' they said. 'Not now. Not tonight.'

But it was too late to stop her, and she told the story of the Piscean boy. He had fulfilled everything that might be expected of somebody with such a birth date: he daydreamed, he wrote poems, he wandered through the streets and fields as though in a daze, he shed tears at the sight of animals in distress, he played the accordion and he fell hopelessly in love with a beautiful girl who could never return his feelings. 'Once a year he would play his accordion in church. I heard it when I was young, and it was as if the music was coming straight from heaven.' She closed her eyes and swayed from side to side, her face transformed for a moment into a picture of serenity before she snapped back into the room. 'But apart from those few minutes each year he was good for nothing. I am afraid to say he died young, at just twenty-two. It was on the day the girl with whom he had been so taken married another man. As the sound of church bells rang through the town he lay on his bed and closed his eyes. The doctor took one look at him and announced that the cause was simple: he had died of a broken heart.'

The old woman looked at the grave faces. 'But all is not hopeless, at least not yet. If my great-great-great-grandchild is a girl then things will of course be easier. We shall make sure her hair matches the somewhat distant look in her eyes, that she grows it long so it tumbles over her shoulders and down her back, and we shall encourage her to paint watercolours and play the harp. There are gentlemen, though I cannot for a moment understand why, who appreciate these somewhat ghostly qualities in a woman, so we can hope she will find a husband who will take care of her. But if you have a son, well . . .' she shook her head, and sat down, '. . . it is in God's hands. All we can do is pray for the child.'

The party never really picked up again after this, and before long everybody had gone away, back to their homes or upstairs to bed.

The young couple tried their best to shrug off what the old woman had said. They told themselves that it was the job of a small town great-great-grandmother to knock three times on the floor with her stick and make doom-laden pronouncements at family gatherings. And besides, suspicions had begun to spread that the old people were losing their touch.

A year before this pronouncement, a bearded vulture had been seen circling above the rooftops, the first time one had been spotted in living memory. The old people knew the town was looking to them to make a declaration about the significance of this event, but they had no idea what to say. Previous generations would have united in a moment, and made an immediate announcement without recourse to conference, deeming it to be a portent of either good or bad fortune, but this generation was flummoxed. Some thought they had a hazy idea of the significance of the last appearance of such a bird, but their memories of the stories they had been told differed significantly from one old person to the next. One said it had presaged a landslide that had wiped out six goats, a mule and an olive tree; another said they vaguely recalled being told that the bird had been a friend to the town, that it had led people into the hills to a hidden ditch where a young boy was lying with a broken leg. Others had differing but equally indistinct memories of stories told to them in childhood by their own grandparents, and it wasn't long before it was accepted that a formal meeting was required. They gathered in the town square, and before a consensus could be reached the vulture was seen once again. Those who had believed it to be a harbinger of good fortune had the opportunity to get a look at its claws and begin to reconsider, and those who had been sure it could only bode ill were struck by its rare grace, and they decided that its presence could, after all, mean that something good was about to befall the town. The discussion went on until nightfall with no conclusions drawn, and when they decided to sleep on it and reconvene in the morning, murmurs began to go around about how old people were not what they used to be.

The ironmonger, a man in late middle age, felt very strongly that this vulture could only be good for the town in general and his shop in particular, and he wished he was old so he could go to the town square and tell them his views on the matter. At three in the morning he shook his wife awake, stood naked before her and declared that he had decided he was old enough. 'Look at me,' he said. 'My hair is silver and my face has enough liver spots. And as for this,' he said, pointing downwards, 'it has certainly changed since our wedding night.' His wife mumbled her agreement and went back to sleep, and in the morning he strode up to the huddle of old people, ready to join in. They fell silent and shook their heads, giving him no choice but to walk away.

With the ironmonger gone, the old people resumed their symposium. Their discussion didn't move on at all from the day before. They knew, though, that patience was running thin and they had to say something before sunset. In the early afternoon, just as they were ready to unite behind a line that the vulture was a straightforward symbol of good fortune to come, the bird returned, flying twice around the town square before swooping on a litter of puppies in a pen behind the ironmonger's shop, taking one of them and flying off, almost low enough for the old people to hit it with their sticks as if it was taunting them with its prize. It flew into the distance until it was just a speck, and then could not be seen at all.

The old people gave up. They declared that the

episode meant nothing more than that a bearded vulture had come to town and had been at once impressive in its majesty and fearsome in its manner, and that while it had been somewhat unfortunate for the ironmonger, there was no further significance to the episode. Even this was not particularly convincing, because now everybody knew that the ironmonger had puppies to sell. There had been a card in his window for a week which had attracted little interest, but their sudden notoriety, combined with the pleading of children who had heard about them and wanted to keep them safe from future bird attacks, ensured that by the end of the day all six that remained had found new homes without a centavo lost to negotiation. The one that had been carried off had been the weakest of the litter, not quite a runt but certainly not a dog that would ever have been likely to sell. The day had ended with the ironmonger satisfied in his prediction, and a creeping sense throughout the town that the old people had lost their touch, that this was the first generation whose minds had been cluttered with television, radio and magazines, so much so that they were no longer able to recall each and every story they had heard as they sat at their grandparents' feet.

It was with this episode in mind that the young couple tried to dismiss the old woman's prediction, but they couldn't keep themselves from hoping that the baby would be born just a fortnight early, that it would be Aquarian, spontaneous and sturdyankled though occasionally a little on the stubborn side, or that it would stay inside just long enough to emerge an enthusiastic and confident, though sometimes impulsive Aries. They reached the middle of February with no sign of labour, and every night, at the great-great-grandmother's suggestion, they kept one of the ovens burning and placed a constantly replenished basket of the most delicious pastries at the foot of the bed in the hope that the smell would prove irresistible to the baby. The child remained unmoved.

The first day of the sign of the fish, came and went without incident, and they knew in their hearts that they couldn't wait another month. Their only hope was that the child would be a girl, but a few days later, in between the births of Mauro and Madalena, the baby arrived. The women of the town leaned over the crib and told the parents how handsome he was, and how one day he would be breaking hearts, glad to be telling comfortable lies about a plain, bald baby, a baby like any other who, they hoped with all their hearts, would grow up to be a man like any other.

The parents vowed never to talk to their child about their worries, but one by one the old woman's predictions came to pass. The first sign was a slightly glazed quality to his eyes, not the empty gaze of the simpleton but the distant look of the dreamer. By this point they had a good idea of what would come next: he would learn a musical instrument and write heartfelt lines of verse.

They never saw his heartfelt verse, and they never mentioned it, but as they passed the door to his room they would often hear the sound of a pen scratching on paper, and of a deep sigh. One year when he was asked what he would like for his birthday he looked to the sky and replied, quietly, 'A euphonium.'

They scoured second-hand shops in nearby towns until they found an instrument they could afford. It was old, and scratched, and its bell a little dented, but the first time their son put his lips to the mouthpiece and blew, the note that came out was at once so clear and so fragile that they felt as if the sky was falling.

One day they saw him standing in the town square, his gaze fixed on a point some way away. They noticed with despair where his eyes were leading him: straight to the town beauty. Straight to Madalena.

They wished his poet's heart could have drawn him to any of the other girls in the town, a girl with whom he would maybe have had a chance, but they all seemed invisible to him. For months the notes he had been playing had seemed to have been chosen at random, but around this time they began to ease into one another to create a sound that was quite extraordinary, and before long the town had become accustomed to the heartbreaking tunes that came from his window every evening as the sun dipped behind the mountain.

★　★　★

Amid all this there was a consolation. Unlike his predecessor, when the time came he was able to hold down a job. He left school at the earliest opportunity to begin his informal apprenticeship in the family trade, and his father was delighted to find that the boy absorbed his expertise with no difficulty. He started by cleaning the ovens and the trays and oiling the machinery, and having proved himself accomplished and reliable in these disciplines he moved on to the baking itself, first just helping his father and doing exactly as he was told, but soon trying his own twists on the family recipes, seeing if there was any way in which he could improve them, and collecting recipes from around the world. Far from drifting in and out of concentration, he focused on his tasks with a single-mindedness that surprised everybody, and it wasn't long before it was generally agreed that he was the finest baker the town had ever known. Even his father was prepared to admit that his young son had superseded him, and he slept soundly at night knowing that when the time came he would be able to hand the business over to him. The boy baked cakes and an extensive range of pastries to a level far beyond that which had previously been considered perfection, but what people talked about more than anything else was his bread. Nobody had ever tasted bread like it, and on market days father and son would have to rise at midnight to get enough ready to meet the demand.

Although he was pleased to know that he was

helping his family's business to thrive, the boy's devotion to his work really had only one motivation: the thought that sometimes something that came from his oven, something he had worked on and worked on until he had got it just right, would be bought by Madalena's mother and would end up on the soft lips, in the warm mouth, and in the sacred belly of the girl he loved. Every once in a while he would catch a glimpse of her as she walked past the shop on her way to or from school, and sometimes she would take a moment to inhale the delicious scents that drifted into the street. And then there were the times when he would see her walking past with a boy, a boy taller than he was, and much, much more handsome. And whenever this happened she didn't seem to notice the bakery. It was as if the sweet tastes within, and the scent that wafted outside, meant nothing to her. Nothing at all.

As the young baker's reputation grew, the mothers of the other local girls wished he would stop looking only at Madalena and notice their daughters instead. He was a pleasant young man, always ready with a smile and a joke as he served customers or made his rounds of the town on his bicycle. A lot of their daughters thought along the same lines. They knew he wasn't nearly as handsome as Mauro, but then nobody was. There was no question that he would make a good husband for some lucky girl, if only he would give up his impossible love for Madalena. The sound of his euphonium drifting through the evening air told them he could never let go of her, and one by one the girls, and their mothers, began to look elsewhere.

One summer day, hearing that Madalena was soon to leave town to study in the city, he approached her as she sat alone in the town square. They had encountered one another at school, and had exchanged pleasantries across the bakery counter, but they had never really had a conversation. She knew, though, what he felt in his heart. Time and again she had seen the love in his eyes, and she longed for the day when he would find somebody else to adore, somebody who could love him in return, but as he sat beside her she saw that his devotion was as steadfast as ever. He opened a paper bag and offered her a jam doughnut. With a smile and a gesture, she declined it.

'Please,' he said, still holding the paper bag towards her.

This time she accepted it, and took a bite. It was delicious. At first it had a crispness to it, then it softened and seemed to turn into a light syrup that slid down her throat, as smooth as water from a mountain spring. 'You are a wonderful baker,' she said.

'Thank you.'

She tried to find some words of comfort. 'One day you'll make your wife very happy.'

He shook his head, and began the speech he had

been planning for so long. He told her he loved her, but from the very start he had known that he had no chance of her returning his feelings. He wished her every happiness. 'There will always be a gap in my life, but it's a gap I will treasure.'

'You'll find somebody else,' she said. 'I just know it.'

He smiled sadly, and shook his head. Madalena knew he was right. He would never find anybody who would make him feel the way she made him feel. Just as the thought of Mauro made every cell in her body dance, he would have felt the same way about her. Mauro returned her love though, and she could only imagine how she would feel if he didn't, if he had fallen not for her but for one of the other girls in the town. She wished there was something she could do to make things better for the young baker, but she felt helpless.

'I will never be a bother to you, Madalena,' he said, 'but I am going to ask just one thing.'

She didn't say anything. She dreaded what he was going to ask of her.

'Wherever you are in the world, when you find your-self breathing in the smell of baking bread will you, just for a moment, think of me? I don't expect you to think of me with love, but if you could think of me with just a small measure of fondness . . . Will you do this for me, Madalena?'

She nodded. He was not asking too much. She loved the smell of baking bread, and she could never think ill of this boy who had done her no harm. She wished she could offer him further words of hope, but she knew it would be for nothing. 'I will,' she said. 'And I'm so sorry.'

The young baker saw the girl's boyfriend approaching. 'Here,' he said, offering her the paper bag. 'Take the rest of them. Share them with your friend.' He wished he could have made his way through life without knowing the name of the boy who had captured the heart of the only girl he could ever love, but in a town this small it was impossible, and there was no point in pretending otherwise. 'Share them with Mauro.'

Madalena took them without a word, and the young baker stood up and walked away.

Mauro arrived, and sat beside her. 'What was that all about?'

Madalena cast her eyes down. 'Oh, nothing really.'

But he knew. He had not been oblivious to the emotions that lay behind the sound of the young baker's euphonium, and he too felt sorry for him. They watched him until he was lost from view.

Madalena offered a doughnut to Mauro. He took a bite, and raised his eyes to the sky. 'Unbelievable,' he said. He took another bite, and shook his head. 'How can anything taste so good?'

They sat under the tree, and for a long time neither said a word.

VII

His working day over, the old man sat alone at his kitchen table. He cut a thin slice from the cake, put it on a plate and stared at it for a while before eating it much as a heron eats a fish: from a state of near stasis erupted a single lightning motion, and it was gone. He cut another slice and ate it in the same manner, then did the same again. He knew that before long the whole cake would be inside him, that he would spend some time staring at the empty tin. But for now it was there in front of him, and it might as well have been the only thing in the world. He was struck by everything about it: by the way it looked, by its aroma, and by its texture both on his fingers and in his mouth. But what he liked most of all about Pavarotti's wife's cake was its delicious taste.

PART TWO

I

A time will come when the doctor's house is a rogue landmark, attracting traffic from all over the city and beyond. Some drivers will slow to a crawl, trying to appear as if they are looking for a house number and have no idea that there is anything exceptional about the street, while others will come to a shameless halt and get out to take photographs. When the place is no longer considered a crime scene and the police have gone away, people will arrive after dark to climb over the fence and explore the garden. By then it will be an earthy wasteland, every inch having been excavated to a depth of at least three metres, and the visitors will leave with their pockets stuffed with souvenir pebbles and splinters of wood. There will be no formal objections when the house, already denuded by the investigation, is pulled down and the ground rolled flat.

For now though, it looks like any of the houses in this part of the city, its paintwork just as shiny, its roof as free of moss and its driveway as well-swept, but for the doctor's neighbours it stands apart. To them it is not so much a home as a monument to his quiet bravery.

The doctor had chosen the house without thinking a great deal about why he had done so, and it was only when he moved in and saw how little room his packing crates took up that he realised the absurdity of living alone in such a large place. He knew at once that he should have bought a cottage or an apartment, but he did nothing to correct his mistake, and he soon stopped paying attention to the doors that led to empty rooms.

Every so often he would encounter an attractive fellow doctor at a conference, or a charming divorcee at a social function, and would begin to wonder whether he was ready to let somebody into his life, somebody with whom he could fill the space that surrounded him. He would sigh, but before this sigh was over he would see an image of Ute glaring at him, challenging him to love the other woman more than he loved her, and every time her victory was immediate and absolute.

At least he has Hans to keep him company, his neighbours said to themselves, as they passed by. *It would be terrible to think of him alone in there with all his memories.*

★   ★   ★

Doctor Fröhlicher was on his second Hans. He had bought the first one to surprise his bride shortly after they had returned from their honeymoon, hoping that a puppy would help make their apartment feel like a home. On seeing the tiny black Labrador looking up from its basket, Ute had narrowed her eyes and said, 'You're not expecting *me* to look after that thing?' This was not the reaction he had been wishing for, and quietly he told her that he would be the one to feed and exercise the animal. Thinking it might bring his wife and the dog closer together, he had asked her what she would like him to be called, and without a moment's hesitation she gave her reply. He hadn't dared ask her why she had chosen that name, and as the possibilities assaulted him he berated himself for allowing the terror to take hold.

'Hans,' he said. 'A fine name.'

In time Ute found it would sometimes suit her to pay attention to Hans, flamboyantly petting him while her husband looked on, and taking him for walks, returning hours later. When the doctor asked where they had been she would only say, 'Out.'

When this first dog had arrived in the city he had a greying muzzle and a touch of stiffness to his legs, and although he had carried on for a few years, it was no great surprise when one morning the doctor had gone downstairs to find his companion's heart had stopped beating in the night. As news of the dog's passing spread through the streets the doctor's patients

75

said, *If only he was a vet – maybe then he could have saved poor Hans.* A few months later he bought a second black Labrador puppy, which he also called Hans, and it was with relief that people agreed that black Labradors are all more or less the same, and one can quite efficiently be replaced with another. *If only*, they thought, *the same could be said of wives.*

As usual the doctor had risen early. He stood in the kitchen, waiting for his Fair Trade coffee to cool and scratching Hans behind the ears. 'It's just as delicious as ordinary coffee,' he said to the dog, 'and what better way to start the day than with a good deed?' He was about to start preparing breakfast when the telephone rang. He had not heard from the old man for some weeks, but he knew it would be him. He answered.

'Oh dear,' he sighed, smiling. Hans looked up at him as the conversation continued, its template familiar. The doctor put down the phone, and told the dog he would be returning before long. He put his stethoscope around his neck, picked up his portmanteau and walked through to the car.

Summer had begun, and it was starting to get light as the garage door opened, and then the gates, and he drove towards the museum.

II

The old man had heard nothing, but in the middle of the night he was woken by the familiar sensation of a light, spindly leg on his cold skin. He knew from experience what this meant; that something had happened in the rooms below, something that would need to be dealt with. He felt the spider cross his cheek, then pause for just a moment before darting into the hollow of his mouth. As it thrashed around, frantic as it struggled to find a way out, he trapped it with his tongue, and with his back teeth he ground it to a paste. He swallowed, then extended a thin arm and set his alarm for five o'clock. Moments later the quiet of the room was broken by the rumble of his breath.

The room filled with a furious beep. With a long, grey finger he slid the switch on the alarm clock to *off*, then he rose to his feet, picked up a plastic torch and walked downstairs. There was a familiar faint metallic quality to the air, and his nose led him to Room Nine, where the smell was thick and unpleasant. As was often the case, there was more than just blood to be dealt with. He opened a window to let in fresh air, then went to a utility cupboard where he picked up a pile of old newspapers that he kept for this reason. He placed them on the floor around the body, and went down to the front desk to make his call to the doctor. Twelve and a half minutes later he was fully dressed and standing by the back door.

The knock came precisely on time, and he stood aside as the doctor entered.

They went up to Room Nine, and the doctor stepped onto the damp, dark newspaper and looked down. 'Once again,' he sighed, with a sympathetic smile, 'it seems we are too late.' He looked for a while longer, then turned to the old man and said, gravely, 'My medical opinion is that the unfortunate gentleman is completely dead.' He walked up and down a few times, crouched, and delivered his post mortem, telling the old man what was already apparent – that the deceased had most likely perished at some time in the early hours of the morning as a result of the loss of blood from a series of self-inflicted wounds to the left wrist. He pointed at the knife, which lay beside a display unit on the other side of the room, a smear marking its course. He continued: 'Judging by the aroma emanating from the body it would seem the deceased soiled himself in his final moments.' The people they found had seldom died cleanly. The doctor wondered why this was always left out of films and theatrical productions: surely, he thought, it would be more realistic for Juliet to find Romeo lying in a puddle of his own urine, and for her to vomit all over the Capulet tomb as she sends her body into shock by digging the knife into her heart.

The doctor had come prepared, bringing with him a woollen blanket in which to wrap the body. When that was done they took one end each and carried it down to the back door. After a few hurried words about the importance of breakfast, the doctor checked for passers-by. He gave the *all clear*, and together the men bundled the corpse into the back of the car.

The old man finished cleaning up. The floor was well-sealed, and nothing would seep through to the ceiling below. Wearing a rubber glove, he picked up the stinking newspapers, stuffed them into a bin bag and went back into the cupboard for a mop and bucket. He added cleaning fluid to the water to mask the smell, and when the floor and skirting board were clean of congealing blood he checked the displays, using a handkerchief to wipe off the occasional spot. He looked around to see if anything had been left behind. The knife was still there, but that was all. He picked it up. It looked new, and sharp. He would use it for his cheese. After checking the stairs for his or the doctor's footprints, mopping a few marks as he went, he put the cleaning apparatus away. The smell was fading, but it remained unpleasant. He left the windows open. If Hulda was to ask him why Room Nine's floor was damp he would tell her he had dropped a mug of coffee, that it had gone everywhere and he had mopped it up. If she mentioned that she had found any stray dark spots or smears he would say that a visitor had suffered a sudden violent nosebleed. He had prepared these explanations some time before, but had never yet had cause to use them.

Back in his kitchen he sat down for breakfast, and as he lifted the dry cracker to his mouth he noticed something stuck in the gap between two of his back teeth. He levered it out with his tongue, and transferred it to the tip of a long, grey finger. It was the dark brown leg of the spider that had crawled into his mouth in the early hours of the morning, just as the blood had spilled from the body downstairs. He counted. Five of the seven segments were there: the femur, the patella, the tibia, the metatarsus and the tarsus. Only the coxa and the trochanter, the short sections closest to the body, were missing. The skinny leg was coated in brown hairs, and there at the end of the tarsus, so small it was barely visible, was the spider's claw, perhaps the one that had woken him in the night. He put it back in his mouth, chewed it, and swallowed.

III

The doctor peeled away the blanket, and looked at the body. Hans had come out to greet him, and he told the dog, as he often did, that one of the benefits of mental or emotional collapse is that often there will only be minimal physical symptoms to accompany the inner turmoil. Sometimes, he continued, the person will be overweight or, as in this case, underweight, but in terms of taste either was preferable to somebody who had died after a long and debilitating illness. He was concerned, though, for himself and Hans not to ingest any second-hand poison. They would be unlikely to die from eating the amount that would make it through to the meat, but it would result in them getting upset stomachs, and he didn't want that.

Self-poisoning had become somewhat old-fashioned, but they still had to be careful. One man passed on to him from the museum had apparently overdosed, probably on a narcotic or a commercial painkiller, but he couldn't be sure that he hadn't taken weedkiller or rat poison. The doctor's garden was often visited by cats, and he had lured one into the garage and fed it morsels of the suspect flesh. The animal had started to exhibit a combination of listlessness and nausea, and the doctor had panicked, grabbed the cat by the scruff of the neck and thrown it into the nearest freezer. With a heavy heart he wrote off the man as inedible, and disposed of all but his liver and a hand, meaning to carry out tests on them. He had kept the cat's body for the same reason, but he found he never quite had the time to conduct his investigation, and it remained in the freezer, its body contorted, stuck in the position in which it had finally given up its struggle.

One of the doctor's worries was of dying without having a chance to cover his tracks, and he shivered at the thought of the garage being searched and people concluding that he must have enjoyed having sex with frozen cats. To ensure that this would not happen, he had written *I do not have sex with frozen cats* on a piece of paper, and left it in a drawer in his study. Sometimes he wondered whether this would be enough to combat speculation.

He felt remorseful about what he had done to the cat, even more so when posters went up around the neighbourhood, appealing for its safe return. The doctor knew the family, and one evening he knocked on their door and after a few gentle words of sympathy for their loss he presented them with a kitten. Within hours this act of kindness had entered into legend.

He opened the freezer next to the one with the cat in it, to see if his new acquisition would fit. Inside was the body of a black man, curled up like an apostrophe. He had collected it from the museum some months earlier, and it had made him a little apprehensive. He had never eaten such dark flesh before, and he couldn't help wondering whether it would taste any different from white. Smokier, perhaps. He had been down to the last few steaks of the woman, and before the phone call that morning he had been thinking about preparing the man for consumption, a little angry with himself for feeling so wary. He was a doctor after all, and he knew he ought not to think this way. Now though, he was able to put these thoughts aside. He could leave this leap into the unknown for another day.

He stripped his new body. 'Fortunately, Hans,' he said, 'because of my profession, I am quite accustomed to bad smells.' He turned the man's pockets inside out and found a note, which he put aside to dry. He would read it another time, if it was legible. He put the man's clothes in a bin bag, then unwound his hose and washed off the worst of the mess. The body would just about fit in with the other one. 'The fuller the freezer,' he said to his dog, 'the more energy efficient it is. And as you know, Hans, it would be wrong of us to use more electricity than is necessary.' He braced himself, and lifted the body.

'In you go,' he said. 'In you go with your coloured friend.'

He slammed the freezer shut and went through to the kitchen, where he made himself a fresh mug of coffee and, at last, ate his breakfast.

IV

On his way downstairs the old man went into the room
where he had found the body, and checked that the
smell had gone away. Satisfied that it had, he closed
the windows. At eight fifty-nine he stood in the hallway.
He looked at the second hand on his watch, and when
the time came he opened the front door.

'Good morning,' said Hulda. 'What a pleasant day.'

He said nothing, and as she carried on he went
upstairs to spend some time with the *K* section of a
Danish–German dictionary. He had arrived at the
museum with two cases, one full of clothes and the
other full of dictionaries. On asking him whether he
had made arrangements to have his other belongings
sent on, Pavarotti's wife was surprised to hear that
these cases contained everything he owned. She had
been impressed by his devotion to his continuing

studies, and was not to know that the only reason he read these books was because they sent him to sleep. He was impatient to spend as many hours as possible asleep, or rather not being awake, and any language skills he acquired as he pursued this ambition were incidental.

When he reached the kitchen he sat in a stiff-backed wooden chair, and opened the book on his knee. *Krapyl. Kras. Krat.* It wouldn't be long before the proprietor and her husband arrived, but he was hoping to fit in a short nap. *Kremlolog. Kremte. Kreneleret.* It was not their usual visiting day. Today they would be making a special appearance, to oversee the delivery and assembly of a human skeleton. *Kringle. Kringlet.* Halfway through *Krinkelkroge* the old man fell asleep, still bolt upright and with his eyes wide open. A rattle came from deep inside him, and a long, grey finger marked the point on the page where his mind had shut down.

When all this is over and she finds out what has been going on in her museum, Pavarotti's wife will not be available for comment. Confined to her room, she will be unable to speak for several weeks. Every afternoon at four o'clock Liesl, Chloris, Dagmar and Swanhilde will be marched in by a nanny, and one by one they will offer their hands, and she will squeeze them, and look into their eyes, wishing she could say something, anything, to explain what had happened, why she had become this way. In spite of her condition she will offer the police her full cooperation. Every day four officers, one of them a police musicologist, will carry her to the grand piano in the corner of the room, and she will sit on the stool in her nightdress, staring straight ahead and playing C sharp minor for *yes*, G flat diminished 7th for *no*, and giving a light flourish on the three highest keys for *I don't know*. As time goes on she will begin to spell out words for them, but only if they contain letters no further into the alphabet than G. In this way the investigation will manage to elicit all the information it needs from her, and at no point will she be under suspicion.

In her absence it is her husband who will field the interview requests from the press. The many reporters who speak to him will make note of his gentle manner, his tactful choice of words and his sense of bemusement and dismay at the events that had taken place, and without exception they will notice that he bears a close resemblance to the late tenor. Most of them, keen to make up a word count in a hurry, will mention this likeness in their copy, though one or two will be restrained enough not to refer to it, believing it to be irrelevant to the story. This high-mindedness will be for nothing, as their readers point at the article's accompanying photograph and say to whoever is within earshot, *Look at him. Look at this man. He looks just like Pavarotti. At first I thought it* was *Pavarotti, but it's not*. They will spend the rest of the day singing ear-splitting approximations of 'Nessun Dorma', and for a few weeks sales of the real Pavarotti's CDs will soar.

The skeleton expert was no different. On arriving at the museum and being introduced to its proprietor and her husband, he was struck by the resemblance, and from that moment he could think of him only as *Pavarotti*, and of his wife only as *Pavarotti's wife*. Her name had been eclipsed, to the point of being all but erased, by the extraordinary appearance of her husband.

On being shown the spot where the exhibit was to go, the skeleton expert began to assemble the curtain that the museum had provided. The rail, which stood on casters, was similar to the kind found on hospital wards, but the fabric was thick and, in keeping with the task, black. Pavarotti's wife asked him the usual polite questions about his occupation – *How does one become a skeleton expert?* and *Is it not frightfully harrowing work?* but soon she was stuck for things to say. After a long silence she asked, 'And when will the . . .' She searched for the right thing to say. 'When will the unfortunate materials arrive?'

The skeleton expert gestured towards a blue plastic crate by his feet.

Pavarotti's wife had envisaged the bones being brought separately, inside a large wooden box borne by several solemn-countenanced gentlemen. She had assumed that the crate, casually carried in by the skeleton expert, had contained tools, and she was shocked to think that somebody who until the age of twenty-nine had been a person could end up stacked inside a modestly sized plastic box with freight stickers on the side. 'Oh,' she said. 'Of course.'

She wanted to turn and go, to find somewhere she could be alone and quiet, where she could remember the skeleton in happier times. Even though she had never known him she could invent these memories, and they would be real enough to her. She knew, though, that she would have to wait before she did this, that first she must be welcoming to her guest. She offered him a tour of the museum so he could find out more about the bones' final resting place. She took him along the suggested route, gravely pointing out certain exhibits along the way. He had no idea what to think or what to say as she sat him down in the *Tell Tale Signs* room and played the short film that informed him of behavioural patterns to look out for in his friends and family (*sighing, looking unhappy, talking in a quiet voice, listening over and over again to sad songs*), and showed him around Room Six, *Statistics*, where he looked in silence at the scale model of Golden Gate Bridge, complete with its frequently updated neon display showing how many people had ended their lives there.

When they got to Room Nine, *Cults and Pacts*, the old man was standing sentry in the far corner, something he only ever bothered to do when he knew he was likely to be observed by his employer. Pavarotti's wife was electrified by his professionalism, and swelled with admiration as she saw in him the same qualities that had made such an impression on her the first time they had met, in the corner of the Concourse Exhibition Unit of Bremen International Airport.

V

Lotte Meier was well-known in her home town for her red hair, her blue eyes and the freckles on her face. But more than anything she was known for her cheerful disposition. Everybody who came into contact with her felt their spirits soar, and found themselves smiling with her. *That girl is a ray of sunshine*, they said to one another. She even smiled as she did her homework, as she tidied her room, and as she made her way around the lawn every morning before school, scooping up her three pet Papillon dogs' latest tiny piles of mess. Whenever her hockey team lost a match she would smile her way back to the changing room, thinking how much fun it had been and hoping they would do a little better next time.

What a shame that this won't last, people would think, *that her infectious* joie de vivre *will diminish as she reaches adolescence*, but when her first period arrived, halfway through a Chemistry class, she greeted it with a chuckle as she carefully put down her pipette and made a sprightly dash to the girls' toilet. In the years that followed she faced all the changes in her body and mind with just such a buoyant manner.

When she was fifteen, Lotte was hit by a car. The driver of a BMW failed to stop as she walked over a pedestrian crossing, and the impact hurled her high into the air in an arc of several metres. She landed hard on the tarmac, and as she lay in a heap in the middle of the road, twisted into an unnatural shape, a crowd gathered around her. As they waited for assistance to arrive she made light of her injuries. Her cries of pain were leavened with smiles and laughter, and she told the onlookers that it was nothing, that the doctors would soon make her better, and in the scheme of things there were people far worse off than she was. And besides, she went on, apart from a few scrapes and bruises here and there, and maybe a few broken ribs and a fractured collarbone, her serious injuries were confined only to one of her legs. What if she had landed differently and hurt her head? If you were to look at it that way, she jauntily explained in between yelps of agony, she was the luckiest girl in the world.

Minutes later the ambulance arrived, and a new wave of passers-by supposed the paramedics had taken leave of their senses as they smiled and joked with their patient. But on drawing closer and seeing the face of the girl who was being tended to, the onlookers also began to smile, even as they noticed that her left shin had snapped and the leg was bent at a horrifying angle, and a long, jagged shaft of raw bone was sticking out from a fist-size wound below her knee.

As she lay in her hospital bed she was surprised and delighted by the stream of chocolates, flowers and cards that arrived. It seemed as if the whole town wished her a full and speedy recovery. She was particularly taken aback by the amount of cards from boys, some of whom she had barely spoken to, in which they said all the usual things about how they hoped to see her up and about before too long, but also things she hadn't expected, like, *I don't know what I would have done if you hadn't made it through.*

That's interesting, she thought.

Her shattered bones fused as well as the doctors could have hoped, and shortly after starting back at school, with the slight limp that would never leave her, Lotte discovered she enjoyed kissing very much. She often found herself in the arms of a boy, and these boys would return her smiles and arrive at her door with flowers in their hands and dreams in their hearts. While she found their attentions delightful, they didn't set her heart aflame, and she could see that none of them was going to grow into the man she was sure was out there waiting for her. Whenever she decided that the time had come for them to part company she would tell the boy in such a way that in the moment it seemed to make perfect sense, as if they really *had* come to the end of the line, that it *would* be best for both of them if they were to just be friends, and that he *would* find somebody to replace her, somebody he would love more than he had ever thought possible. It wouldn't be until he got home that he would wonder why he was smiling, and realise that this really was the end, that he would never hold her small, pale hand again, or kiss those freckled lips.

On occasions when she knew a smile would be inappropriate, Lotte's face would go into a state of repose, but she still radiated joy. Even in bereavement her belief in heaven, and in the inherent goodness of the departed, kept her shining as she grieved. And thus she smiled her way through childhood, through university and out into the world, and at the age of just twenty-four she smiled her way into a job as the Head of Concourse Relations at Bremen International Airport.

Lotte's disposition came across not only in person, but also on paper. In her application she said it would be her intention to ensure that the departure area of Bremen International Airport became known not just as a hub of transportation, but also as a hub of cultural activity, a pleasurable and enlightening experience rather than just a waiting room. Although she was by no means alone in this approach, something about her application sent it straight to the top of the pile. The recruitment panel looked at it, then at one another, and nodded. She was called in for an interview, and before she even opened her mouth she had secured the position.

Two weeks later she started work, and by her first coffee break she had got to know her colleagues and organised her desk, and begun to implement her plan. A press release was sent out, announcing that an art gallery was to be established inside the departure area. Everybody who read it found themselves thinking, *What a wonderful idea.*

She spent her days sending letters to various public galleries and private collectors with the intention of securing loans of paintings. Until these letters arrived none of the recipients had any idea that they would be interested in *helping to consolidate the already healthy reputation of Bremen International Airport,* or *showing the world that Bremen is more than just the home of Beck's beer and the birthplace of Hans-Joachim Kulenkampff,* but something made them want to do their bit. Everybody who was able to responded with offers of loans, but even so they would only part with works that they wouldn't miss. Across the land curators scratched their heads and said, *Well, we do have that early Mühlberg in storage, the one he painted before he really found his feet,* or, *We could send her that Rohlfs – the one he disowned because he didn't deem it up to scratch.* In large private houses a typical conversation between husband and wife would find them agreeing that the faint sketches by Ernst Deger that had been hanging in their downstairs lavatory for some years had attracted very little comment from their guests, and that it would be nice to let other people enjoy them for a while.

As each piece arrived Lotte would see only the good in it, and her face would be a picture of delight. And so it was that the Concourse Gallery of Bremen International Airport amassed a collection of pieces of quite stultifying mediocrity.

At the press launch the critics found themselves smiling back at Lotte, and telling her how much they were enjoying the exhibition. In the moment this had not been a lie, but once they had returned to their apartments and switched on their computers they were unable to recall a single point of merit in anything they had seen, and they stared for hours at blank screens. They tried to write down their feelings, but every time they were about to begin, Lotte appeared in their minds' eyes. Across the city, and farther afield, fingers froze on keyboards. They knew they couldn't commend such an exhibition, that to do so would damage their reputations, possibly beyond repair, but at the same time even the hardest-nosed among them knew that they could never live with themselves knowing they had brought even a moment's sadness to that smiling face.

Planned double-page spreads were abandoned, and mentions of the exhibition were relegated to short entries on listings pages, saying things like, *Bremen International Airport will be displaying various artworks inside its terminal building.* Lotte overlooked the bland neutrality of these pieces, and was delighted with the coverage. Once the ribbon had been cut by the mayor, people with time to spare before boarding would see the sign, and go in, and wonder what it was in these pictures that they were supposed to be looking at. And while they were doing this they would be watched by a pair of eyes belonging to an old man, his face a deathly grey.

The pieces, for all their absence of life, were old and unique, and some were the work of artists whose more successful efforts had afforded them some standing; as a result the exhibition had to be insured for a significant sum. After many phone calls, it had become apparent to Lotte that in order to keep the premiums at an affordable level the exhibition would have to be overseen at all times. Even though the paintings were to be hung behind glass screens, the companies still insisted that *a minimum of one human being (extant)* would be required to be on hand whenever the exhibition was open to the public. The airport was as secure as any other (every morning on the way to her office the pins in Lotte's leg set off the metal detector and she smilingly yielded to the formality of the frisking), but even so it was impossible to find a policy, which did not include such a stipulation.

As the exhibition was being set up she had stood in the gallery as an insurance broker, immaculately suited and as tiny as a jockey, set about explaining the finer details of risk assessment. 'There can be no under-estimating the wiliness of the art thief,' he had said, taking his silk handkerchief from his pocket and lightly dabbing his forehead. 'They appear as if from nowhere, and then . . .' The handkerchief disappeared. He opened his palms to show that he wasn't concealing it there. Lotte was delighted. 'And, Miss, as you know, this is an international airport, and at any moment there could be any number of Norwegians passing through, which puts under-guarded artworks at *enormous* risk of being whisked away in an audacious smash-and-grab raid.' He pointed at his breast pocket and now the hand-kerchief was there, but the next moment it was gone again. Lotte laughed. 'But the Norwegians are not the only ones we need to be wary of. Maniacs from anywhere – from as far afield as Angola, or Ireland, or from as close as this very city,' he made a circular gesture, 'could come here with Cuban heels and mischief in their minds.' He walked to the far side of the room, and his affable manner was abruptly replaced by bug-eyes and bare teeth as he took off his shoe and with a blood-curdling howl ran forward and mimed a Cuban-heel attack on the glass that had been put in place to protect a painting of the staggeringly plain wife of a nineteenth-century textile merchant. His was a handmade Italian business shoe, and his demonstration was executed so faultlessly that at no point did it touch the glass, but he was so convincing that Lotte agreed with no further discussion that the insurance companies were right. Cameras would not be enough.

She decided this would be preferable anyway, because with somebody on duty at all times people would be able to ask questions about the pieces and receive informed replies. An advertisement for the positions of Gallery Attendant and Chief Gallery Attendant was placed in an appropriate periodical, and a small number of applications was received.

The first appointee, the Gallery Attendant, was a keen graduate of an arts administration course, who had been looking for a foothold in a competitive profession. The next, nominally the graduate's superior, even though barring a very small amount of paperwork their day-to-day roles were identical, was a man who had come with several years of experience, having moved from a railway museum in Prüm. He was quite an old man, and his long, grey fingers hung like stalactites from the sleeves of his funereal jacket.

There was nothing to do but stand still. Normally the role of Gallery Attendant, or indeed that of Chief Gallery Attendant, will include answering questions about the pieces from the visitors or, more usually, directing them to the toilets, but here it was different. This being an airport, toilets were abundant and clearly signposted, and the works themselves invited little explanation, even the short paragraphs on the mounted cards seeming excessive under the circumstances. The keen graduate, exhausted by the procession of disappointed faces, soon found work elsewhere, and was replaced by another keen graduate, who also left at the first opportunity.

The old man, though, remained. Working in an unpopular museum or gallery was as close to getting paid for being unconscious as it was possible to get, and because of his exceptional language ability he never had any difficulty finding such a position. The owners always imagined their establishment being visited by people from around the world, and they were keen to employ a polyglot. They didn't realise that he would go to great lengths to avoid conversation in every language in which he was fluent. Lotte too had been impressed by his gift, though it was only ever used when eavesdropping on visitors, most of whom would say little besides, *These paintings are certainly preferable to that modern rubbish.* But as the words came out these visitors began to wonder whether what they were saying was true. If all the old days had to offer was a painting of an unimaginably ordinary windmill then maybe there *was* something to modern art after all.

Lotte's gallery had its own shop. Sometimes a restless traveller waiting for a delayed flight would drop in and, for a minute or two, look around. Baffled by the sight of its lacklustre ashtrays, ceramic pencil sharpeners, tea towels and place mats, they would go away without having felt any inclination to buy anything. For a long time the closest the shop came to making a sale had been when a flustered man had rushed in and picked up a mug. He didn't look at the picture on it, but if he had done he would have seen a particularly non-descript landscape by Georg Friedrich Ackermann, one that on close inspection could be seen to be quite badly water damaged. Without even looking for the price, the man had handed over a credit card. The girl behind the counter looked at the till, then at the card, then back at the man.

'Please hurry,' he said. 'My plane is boarding, and I need to buy this mug as a gift for my estranged daughter.'

The girl stared at the till. It had been so long since her training that she had forgotten which buttons she needed to press.

'Please,' said the man. His voice had begun to wobble. 'My estranged daughter . . . She will be waiting for me . . . It is imperative . . .'

The girl looked once again at the card, then back at the till, and at the man before saying, 'I'm sorry, sir.' She handed the mug and the card to him, and whispered, 'Just go.'

The man took the mug, stuffed the card back into his wallet and hurried towards his departure gate. The girl watched him rush away, wondering how things would go with his estranged daughter, what she would think about meeting her father after such a long time and being handed such a disappointing mug.

He had been their only customer until the day a woman had come in and bought at least one of everything, a woman whose build made it difficult to tell whether or not she was expecting a baby, even though she was five months pregnant with her third child, who would be a girl called Dagmar.

Before reaching the shop, Pavarotti's wife had gone to the exhibition, where she had scrutinised each of the exhibits with genuine interest. When she got to the man standing in the corner, instead of shuffling past and deliberately avoiding eye contact as every previous visitor had done, she looked at him very closely, as if he too was on display.

'Sir,' she said, 'what a wonderful little exhibition you have here.'

The old man accepted the praise with a nod.

'I congratulate you.'

Indifferent to her approval, and waiting for her to go away, he felt no need to nod for a second time.

'I suppose you are incredibly experienced in the field of curatorship and so forth?'

He nodded.

'So tell me, where were you before you came here, to this splendid concourse gallery?'

The old man began to wonder whether there might

be a reason beyond nosiness for this interrogation so, in as few words as possible, he replied. He told her he had come from a railway museum in Prüm. He didn't mention that the museum had been a shambles, that it hadn't even contained a train and that it had failed quite disastrously, the premises being sold off by creditors and converted into a restaurant called Pippin's, themed around the story of Pippin the Hunchback.

'And before that?'

He told her, in as few words as possible, about his time at the Wolfsburg Museum of Recent Local Architecture, the Bad Neustadt Handball Experience and the Regensburg Reformation World of Teddy Bears. He could have listed more, but chose not to. It was none of her business, and he was not yet sure whether she had anything to offer him.

The woman's eyes narrowed in curiosity. 'Why have you moved around such a lot?'

'Because I have been wishing to gain the broadest possible experience in the field.' This was the line he always gave at job interviews, and he was able to say it without thinking. He chose not to tell her that everywhere he had worked had closed, just as he knew this gallery would close. He had chosen these places carefully, knowing they were hopeless, that he wouldn't be kept busy, and that he might even receive a pay-off when the inevitable end came.

The woman's eyes widened. 'Wonderful,' she said,

and she began to tell him, in considerable detail, about her own plans to open up a museum.

The old man had heard this all before, enthusiastic proprietors outlining ideas for projects which they saw as the centrepiece of a life's work, oblivious to just how ridiculous they would be, and how unpopular. This woman's dream, so passionately set forth, was the most ludicrous he had ever heard. 'I am sure it will be a great success,' he said, when, at last, she stopped to draw breath.

She told him that she would be looking for somebody to oversee it, somebody with a broad range of appropriate experience. 'A chief attendant if you will.' She thought for a moment. 'No, let us say *a curator*.'

The old man said nothing.

'Oh, you must forgive me,' she said. 'I am being indiscreet. Here you are in your current employment, and I am making what could almost be described as overtures to you. What an awful breach of protocol on my part.'

'Not at all, madam.' Now certain that these were indeed overtures, he began to wonder whether he should take up her offer. He was tired of the airport's security procedures and the incessant drone of announcements, and he could sense the gallery's imminent failure. He was sure he would soon be looking for a new position.

'I was about to tell you the terms of employment, about how an apartment on the top floor would be included, and so on and so forth. How indiscreet of me. You have maintained your composure quite admirably throughout this rather awkward encounter.' Her face burned, and the old man could see that her embarrassment was genuine. 'I am so very sorry.'

'Not at all.' He particularly liked the idea of the apartment. He disliked having to deal with landlords, and having to travel to and from work. 'Perhaps you could give me your details, and at some point we could enter into an informal communication on the matter.'

She took a card from her wallet, and pressed it into his hand before taking her leave. She went into the shop, and her eyes lit up. A few minutes later she walked away with three bulging bags.

The girl behind the counter, who by this point had relearned how to work the till and had covered the cost of the flustered man's mug from her own wages, picked up the telephone and called Lotte, who darted out from her office to look at the till roll.

'This is wonderful,' she said, her face even more ablaze with joy than usual. 'Things are really starting to take off.'

Things did not take off. The spree had come too late, and the following day all the gallery staff were called into a meeting where they found themselves confronted by somebody they had never seen before, a stern-looking man in incredibly dark glasses. A deep scar, running diagonally across his right cheek, gave the impression that he had once fought a tiger, and won. When they were all seated he told them that a decision had been made. The exhibition had not done as well as had been hoped, and it was going to be dismantled and replaced by a four-times-life-size waxwork of Hans-Joachim Kulenkampff. 'The largest of its kind,' he said.

The airport's senior management had known they would be unable to break bad news to Lotte, so they had hired this man, supposedly the toughest freelance firer in the business, to do the job for them. For his sake they had made him wear the glasses, which were completely opaque, so he would never know the face to which he was bringing such disappointment. He considered this insulting, but as they were paying him very well he had not protested. As he spoke his prepared lines he began, for the first time ever, to feel awful about what he was doing, and thankful that the young woman they had told him about was hidden from view. As he stared at the blackness in front of him he found himself wondering whether he was in the right job.

Lotte's face continued to radiate joy as she searched for the good in this situation – good which she knew would be there somewhere. The girl from the shop reached into her sleeve and pulled out an extraordinarily large handkerchief, almost a tablecloth, and began to cry, and the old man's latest junior looked quietly at the floor, despondent at her career having hit such a low so early on. Lotte realised that her dream had come to nothing.

'I have let everybody down,' she said. Her eyes twitched, and a tear ran down her cheek, and for the first time in her life she put her head in her hands. 'All you good people,' she choked into her palms, 'I have let you down.'

The man had memorised his exit route, and without even giving them his scripted valediction – *The airport wishes you every success in the future* – he stood up and walked to the back of the room before anybody had a chance to see that Lotte's tears had been infectious. As he passed her he caught a glimpse of her face through the gap in the side of his glasses, and this moment, just a fraction of a second, was enough to knock him off balance. He felt his legs buckle, and he miscounted his steps and walked into a stationery cupboard, where he remained. In the darkness he resolved to go straight home and call his brother, who had given him an open invitation to join his business making lavender bags deep in the countryside. At the time he had struggled to stop himself from turning crimson with fury and calling his brother all sorts of names, but now he could see it was the only option left to him, and he was grateful for it.

As the sobs continued, the old man reached into his wallet, and with the tips of two long, grey fingers picked out the woman's card. He had a call to make.

*   *   *

To begin with, the press will have difficulty tracking down images of the old man, and it will be the photograph from his airport identification card that stares out from the front pages of newspapers. By this time Lotte, whose sunshine had quickly returned, will be two successful jobs down the line, and she will remember him with a shiver. 'He was never very nice,' she will say to her husband, who will not have heard her speak like this before. She will remember the time she had spent with him, and how she had always given him the benefit of the doubt, just as she had given so many people the benefit of the doubt. She will go to her computer and pull up the reference she had written, the one that had secured him the job. He was *punctual*, she reads. *Reliable. A highly valued member of the team. A pleasure to work alongside.* They read like the words of somebody who is not very bright, who sees the world only as it ought to be, and from that day something about her will change. There will be times when she will seem distracted, as if her mind is on something quite serious, and on occasion her brow will crease, as if she is trying to decipher a code. Sometimes she will look at a situation and not be able to find the good in it, and sometimes, just sometimes, she will even look at a person and not be able to find the good in them. She will be aware of this change, and feel grateful for it. She is going to be a mother, she tells herself. It's time she grew up. Her husband will notice this shift, and he will be glad of it too: it had become quite exhausting being married to a ray of sunshine.

When Lotte calls the police they take her details, and at the end of their short conversation she tells them they are welcome to get back in touch with her if there is anything else they need to know.

They do not call. There is nothing else they need to know.

VI

Doctor Fröhlicher had always known that he would practise medicine for as long as he was able. Whenever he attended a fellow doctor's retirement party he couldn't help picturing the massed ranks of the unwell upon whom they were turning their back, and he knew he could never do the same. He was determined to remain at the forefront of the profession, and most evenings he would settle down in an armchair with a medical journal to read about all the latest advances. If things had turned out differently this would have been the time he spent with his wife and family, and by filling it this way he was able to reassure himself that Ute had not died in vain, that in her passing she had helped him to reach new heights as a general practitioner. Whenever he prescribed a medicine that he might otherwise not have known about, or referred somebody to a specialist whom he had read was in the vanguard of their field, it was as if they were working as a team, and when the patient left his consulting room he would close his eyes, and say, 'Thank you, Ute.'

He often imagined how she would have looked. In his mind's eye she had a few lines on her face, and she wore reading glasses, but she was still slim and had kept her hair long, and she remained the most beautiful object he had ever seen. She would have calmed down by now too. There would have been none of her nonsense, not any more.

For all his dedication, the doctor's medical ambitions were hampered by a recurring problem. His patients felt duty-bound to lift his spirits, and on entering his consulting room they greeted him cheerfully, and engaged him in lively chatter about very little. When the small talk ran out and the time came for them to present their symptoms, they began to feel uneasy. The pain in their thumb that may or may not have been the onset of arthritis seemed too trivial to mention when compared with the agony this man went through every day; the small patch of darkening skin that had kept them awake with worry became insignificant in the presence of such forbearance. They declared that whatever it was that had been troubling them had suddenly got better. *It is as if just being here in your consulting room has cured me,* they said.

He would ask them if they were sure, and they would insist that there was nothing wrong, that they had just been feeling a little under the weather but now they were fine. If he noticed that in spite of their protestations they looked ill, or anxious, he would insist on an examination, and he always found the root of the problem. This way he gained a reputation for being very thorough. Often, though, he took them at their word and let them go away, but never until they had assured him that they would make another appointment the moment they began to feel unwell again. Sometimes when the patient did finally return and admit their symptoms it would be too late, and all he could do was make sure that they were kept as comfortable as possible until the end.

Nobody ever railed on their deathbed that *It was the doctor – he should have seen the warning signs.* No grieving husband or wife ever came after him with a team of lawyers. Instead they sighed, and said he had done everything he could. When the television cameras arrive his patients will queue up to say just how dependable he had appeared to be, and how capable and kind, and how the news had come as such a shock.

He sat behind his desk and waited for his first patient of the afternoon, a Frau Irmgard Klopstock, one of the many middle-aged women on his books. As she sat down she started talking, red-faced, about how pleasant the weather had been, and how her garden had really come to life. Once this was over the doctor asked her why she had come to see him, and she told him how ashamed she felt for having troubled him, because the pain she had been feeling had gone away. 'It is as if just being here in your consulting room has cured me,' she said.

He had noticed something awkward about the way she walked in, and decided to press her. 'Tell me anyway,' he said, 'before it went away, where was this pain?'

Frau Klopstock turned an even brighter red, and he gave her his gentle *You can tell me, I'm a doctor* look. In a trembling whisper, she told him. He smiled. She was relieved that he had pressed her, that she had finally told somebody other than her husband about this problem. She felt a weight lift from her shoulders, and was thankful for having such a wonderful family doctor.

He reached into his desk drawer for his camera. 'Now,' he said, reassuringly, 'for medical purposes I am going to take a few photographs of the affected area. Frau Klopstock, please would you remove your . . .' He gestured.

She did as he asked.

Doctor Fröhlicher smiled. With the new addition to his freezer the day had started well, and it kept getting better.

VII

As he worked, the skeleton expert was grateful for the black curtain that surrounded him, because it stopped him from having to see the *Harsh Realities* room's other exhibits every time he looked up from his work. To one side was a papier-mâché dummy of a woman in a bath, the water made from red Cellophane and her mouth hanging open as her eyes bulged and her sky blue head rolled backwards, and to the other side hung a series of photographs, blown up and mounted on canvas, of the shattered body of a Seoul stock-broker who, on seeing some unfortunate numbers appear on a screen, had hurled himself from a very high window. He was glad that this job would only last for one day.

The skeleton expert heard few footsteps. He was

not surprised. He had no idea why anybody would want to visit a place like this.

As the museum closed for the day, Hulda returned to make sure the area around the new exhibit was left clean. She made two cups of coffee and took them to Room Seven. She pulled aside the black cotton, and as the coffee cooled she watched the skeleton expert attach the feet. She tried to let him do his job in peace, but it was impossible. Only by speaking, or singing, or humming, could she keep her most horrifying memories and her most petrifying visions of the future at bay. She could feel them creeping up on her, and urgently needing to fill the silence, she asked the skeleton expert all the questions he had come to expect from such encounters. As he gave his customary replies she found herself becoming fascinated, and in her subsequent questions she delved a little deeper, asking how the bones were prepared. He told her all about the ammonia, and the beetle larvae. After a few more technical questions, Hulda asked about the bones' history.

He worked on as he told her what little he had learned from the skeleton's executors. It had all been quite straightforward. Before he died, the skeleton had given a reason for his decision, one which people had been ready to accept: there had been a woman who had decided she didn't want him after all, and he had believed he couldn't live without her. The case could have come from a textbook, the only deviation being his request for his bones to be preserved.

Hulda noticed that, like all skeletons, it seemed happy. Inside all of us, she reflected, were smiling bones. She would do her best to remember from now on that even on the hardest days there was always a smile underneath her skin. She made a mental note to report this thought to Pavarotti's wife, to let her know that the new exhibit had already brought inspiration to a troubled soul.

She still wished with all her heart that the skeleton had held on and waited for things to get better. She had held on. It had been hard, at times excruciating, but she was glad she had. Silence descended, and as steam rose from the coffee, she felt as if she and the skeleton expert were exchanging sad stories around a camp fire, and that it was now her turn to take the floor. She started telling him about her stepfather, and as her story went on he found he could no longer concentrate on his work. He put his tools aside, picked up his mug and listened in horror.

She didn't tell him everything, not by a long way, but she gave him a flavour of what her life had been like for those years, how it had felt for her to be woken by the scratch of a moustache and a blast of breath that smelled of beer and pickled onions. She told the skeleton expert that at the end of one particularly awful night, when her stepfather had at last left her alone, she had cursed God for having allowed such things to happen to her. 'You should have heard some of the names I called Him,' she said, her face grave. 'I shock myself just thinking about it, but at the time I was very angry, and I didn't know who else to blame. The Father, the Son and the Holy Spirit, well, I am afraid all three of them came in for quite a scolding.'

Although such an outburst had only happened once, she knew that had been enough. She had committed the only unforgivable sin, and from that moment, no matter how she lived the rest of her life and no matter how much she prayed for salvation, she was destined to spend eternity in the fires of Hell. 'I can't even say that I didn't really mean it,' she said, 'because I meant it with all my heart. It's a pity that God can't forgive me, but I do understand that rules are rules.'

The skeleton expert had no idea what to say. He wondered whether he should tell her she was wrong, that when she died she would not go to Hell because there was no such place, and there was nothing awaiting her. He stopped himself. He didn't want to disparage her faith, and besides, he only *hoped* he was right. It was so much easier to think that there was nothing waiting for him than it was to face the alternative.

'Please do not make this mistake,' she said.

He could see how much this meant to her so he nodded, but it was too late. Without even thinking about it he had said such unholy things more times than he could remember, and if any of this was true he was in serious trouble. He tried not to think about it as he drank the last of his coffee, thanked her for it and went back to his tools. He was relieved when she took the empty mugs and stood up, but she had not finished.

'But of course,' she said, 'it is important for me to remind myself that I must not end up as this poor gentleman has, that I must do all I can to stay alive for as long as possible. Otherwise what would I be doing but playing straight into the Devil's hands?'

The skeleton expert said nothing, and Hulda, her brow furrowed and her head bowed, went away.

At seven o'clock Pavarotti, Hulda, Pavarotti's wife and the old man stood in a row, waiting for the skeleton expert to make his final adjustments. After some almost invisible changes with some very small tools, he straightened up and stepped aside.

Pavarotti's wife was the first to examine the new addition to the museum. She looked the bones up and down, and spoke the words she had prepared.

'Friend,' she said, 'in death you shall be of service to others. Through you they will see what a terrible mistake they would be making if they were to follow the same path.' She reached into her enormous bag and pulled out a display card on a stand. At the top was the dead man's name, and underneath, in four languages, was a single-sentence summary of his history. He had been heartbroken, it said, and seeing no hope of happiness he had hanged himself. There was a pictorial invitation to examine the crack in his vertebra, and in the bottom corner of the card was a photograph, provided by the man's relatives, of him in happier times.

The room was silent but for Hulda's sobs. She was heartbroken for the skeleton, but also angry with him for having done what he had done. Looking at the photograph she could see at once that she could have loved him, but now it was too late. He had chosen to die rather than find her and spend his life with her. Her sobs were fuelled by a swell of self-pity, and the shame that came with it. Pavarotti's wife put a hand on her shoulder.

Slowly Hulda pulled herself together. As the world around her came back into focus she saw that Pavarotti was looking directly at her, his eyes full of concern. Her heart sped up, and she wondered whether this would be a good time to ask him if he had a brother. Before she had a chance, his wife started speaking to the skeleton again, and the moment was gone.

VIII

Hans looked up at his master with expectant eyes. Two thick steaks overlapped on the plate, and the doctor was already thinking about frying a third for dessert. He cut off a fatty chunk, and threw it high. Hans leapt up and caught it, and the doctor, his cheeks round with meat, explained that with the new addition to the freezer they could allow themselves a little overindulgence as they finished what remained of the woman they had been eating for such a long time. He always got as much use from each body as he could, and as he refined his butchery techniques less and less went to waste, but there were still a few parts he would never eat. Armpits repulsed him and went straight into the bin, and the thought of putting another man's penis in his mouth, no matter how well-disguised by sauce, made him shudder. He had no qualms about feeding male genitalia to Hans, though. He had known effeminate dogs, and hoped the testosterone would help ensure he never went down that route.

Sitting beside the steak was something he had been saving: one of the woman's kidneys. He sliced into it, and could taste it before it had even reached his mouth. As always, it reminded him of the first time.

Doctor Fröhlicher had started eating people in his first year at the hospital. At a particularly messy post mortem he had, without asking himself why, slipped a kidney into his pocket. When he got home the apartment was empty. Ute and Hans were out on one of their walks, and straight away he cut it into slices, fried it, and put it on a plate alongside a chunk of bread and a spoonful of his favourite mustard. It had tasted much like any kidney he could have bought from a butcher's shop, the only difference being that it was much, much better. The feeling that surged through his body reminded him of the moment his hands had first cupped Ute's breasts. Just like that time, as soon as it was over he could think of nothing but how he could find this feeling again. While he had been preparing the meat he had told himself that he was doing this only out of idle curiosity, that all doctors must try it at one time or another, but as soon as the food was in his mouth he knew why he had really done it, and he knew that it had worked. As he chewed, he no longer wondered where his wife was, or what she might be doing. The meat had given him a respite from the nagging pain of his desperate love, but once it had been swallowed and the taste had faded, all the usual fears rose up before him once again, and he struggled to drive them away.

From that day he would take every opportunity to pocket an off cut from an autopsy, or furtively slice a wedge from an amputated limb. When Ute was gone the nature of his pain changed but he found he needed this relief more than ever, and as his hunger intensified he brought home more and more. With this habit came the worry that at any moment he might be discovered, and lose his licence, and no longer be able to cure people, and sometimes fear and a burning shame took over and he would look Hans in the eye and vow to stop. In the moment he meant this absolutely, but as soon as the next opportunity presented itself the vow would be forgotten.

One afternoon a nurse had come close to catching him as he hid a liver in his briefcase, and in that moment he could see what he was doing. He was losing control of himself, and he knew he had to put this behind him. He decided that the only solution would be to remove himself from the temptations of the hospital. He moved into general practice, hoping that his daily duties would keep him detached from any possibility of a relapse, and for years this worked. His shame receded, but the agony remained, and with it the knowledge that all he would ever need to give himself a respite from it would be a mouthful of illicit meat.

One morning the phone rang, and the doctor went to the museum to attend to a girl that the old man had found in Room Six, moaning as she lay next to a puddle of vomit, an empty bottle of aspirin by her side.

Doctor Fröhlicher had been Pavarotti's wife's family doctor since he had moved to the city. She considered him to be the museum's doctor too, and had given the old man his home and work numbers, telling him to call straight away should he or any visitor ever need medical assistance.

That day he had crouched over the woman, and listened to her heart with his stethoscope. He gave her a glass of water and made sure she drank it all before sending her on her way, his mind racing the whole time. When she was gone he explained to the old man that he would not fill in any paperwork, that to do so would draw attention to this episode and might damage the reputation of the museum.

'For the sake of the nerves of the proprietress,' he said, 'I think it would be best if you were always to call me in the first instance, even if the prospective patient appears to be in an advanced state of . . . no longer being alive. There will be no need for an ambulance, or any of that silliness. We are both gentlemen of the world, so let us keep such incidents between ourselves.' He looked hard at the old man, and had a feeling that they understood one another. He smiled, and said, 'Until the grave.'

The old man nodded. He had no interest in telling

anybody about what had happened. He just wanted to clear up the mess in Room Six, and forget the incident had ever occurred.

The doctor went away, his heart racing. He felt torn in two, one part hoping that he would never hear from the old man again, and the other almost feverish with anticipation. Three weeks later his telephone woke him once again, and the moment he heard the familiar voice he knew what had happened, and he knew what he would do.

He struggled to avoid showing the old man how much he was trembling as he was invited in through the back door. This time he could tell at a glance that the person he had rushed over to treat was quite dead, and it was the same the next time, and the next.

The old man could see that the doctor was acting unconventionally, but he had no cause for concern. All that mattered to him was that his own hands were clean, and he had fulfilled his duty by contacting a medical professional. If that medical professional then chose to bundle the body into the back of his car and drive away at high speed it was hardly his concern. He wasn't going to tell a doctor how to do his job.

Carefully categorised receipts found by the police in a filing cabinet at the doctor's home will reveal that around this time he had made a visit to a kitchen goods store, where he had bought a second chest freezer, a large refrigerator and a selection of steel hooks.

* * *

With two complete bodies in the garage, Doctor Fröhlicher could see weeks, even months, ahead, and just knowing that at any time he could go to the fridge and cook some meat was enough to keep the torment at arm's length. Feeling how different life could be with a regular supply, he had grown determined never to go without again. He felt sad for these people, though. Had they walked into his clinic he would have done everything in his power to help them, but they had not; by the time they came into his life each one of them had made their final decision, and it was too late for him to help them. He was sure, though, that they would all have been happy to know that even though they were gone, they were still helping him, a general practitioner, to get through the day.

There had been times when his reserves had run low and he could feel unrelieved despair hovering close at hand, but he wasn't going to worry about that now. The old man would call again before the freezer was empty. He always did. The doctor told himself that everything would be fine, that somewhere in the world there would be somebody so unhappy that they could see no light, and somehow they would find their way to the museum, where they would crumble in defeat.

IX

Mauro and Madalena said goodbye to their families and began the long journey to the city, Madalena with dreams of becoming a pharmacist, and Mauro planning to qualify as an optician. They had spoken of one day returning to the town and opening businesses directly opposite one another, so in quiet moments they could look at one another across the street, and smile. But that was something to think about another time. For now they were too busy trying to hide their nerves as the bus took them away from everything they had known. After just a few minutes it all seemed a world away: the town square, the shops and the faces that had been there all their lives, growing older but somehow remaining just the same. As the bus carried on, down and down, they looked out of the window, their fingers intertwined.

They said very little, each of them hoping they weren't making a mistake.

Their days filled with campus maps, classes and long sessions in libraries, but every evening, when their studies were over, they met up and explored, getting lost in mazes of narrow streets, embracing on bridges, sitting on the steps of grand buildings, looking out for dropped coins and making wishes as they threw them in fountains. They sought out places that sold cheap coffee, and drank it slowly. They were happy just to be together, to do whatever they felt like doing without the thought that their every movement was being monitored by neighbours, aunts and shopkeepers. As the city thundered around them they had never felt so invisible, and their evenings would always end in one of their rooms, their bodies wound together on a single bed as they spent the long hours they had been dreaming of, their kisses slow and their fingers following hitherto unexplored contours on each other's skin.

Madalena found that wherever they went there was something to catch her eye. With so much for her to untangle it was a while before it struck her that a lot of the sights that held her gaze were people. Her eyes would land on somebody walking past, and even though she knew it was impolite to stare she just couldn't look away. It took a while longer for her to realise that the people who were transfixing her were, without exception, women. She had seen women like these on television and in magazines, but they hadn't seemed real. Here, though, they were three-dimensional and they carried their beauty with no apparent effort, as if it was just a simple, ordinary fact.

The men didn't catch her eye nearly so much. They went past in their thousands, but she never saw one who came close to being as handsome as Mauro. One evening, as they sat on the steps of a church, she turned to look at him and noticed that his eyes were also on the passers-by. It seemed that he too was paying the men very little attention. For the first time she was not the only girl he saw. She also noticed that some of these women would see him looking in their direction, and smile just a little before lowering their eyes and carrying on their way.

He turned to Madalena. 'Come on,' he said. He offered his hand and pulled her to her feet. As she smiled up at him her worries faded into the back of her mind, but she could feel them sitting there, ready to jump out again.

She couldn't sleep. As Mauro lay on her bed she sat at her desk, and in the dim light she looked in the mirror. She recalled some of the women who had walked past, with their lustrous hair, slim waists and delicate features, and as she stared at the image that looked back at her she faced the realisation that she was not a great beauty. She wasn't ugly, and neither was she plain: she was a pretty girl, but that was all. She reminded herself of the words that Mauro had spoken to her over the years, and of the vow they had made, and she went back to lie beside him, to lay her head on his chest as it rose and fell. He stirred. She wanted him to wake up and look at her with eyes alight with love, but instead he rolled over and let out a long sigh.

As they walked together Madalena went out of her way to look for girls who were better-looking than she was. She never had to wait very long until a lithe goddess or a golden-haired elf-child passed by, leaving her feeling inelegant and bad at make-up. Sometimes they passed a girl who was trying her best to hide the fear in her eyes, a girl who in her small town or village would have been pretty enough to have been considered *very* pretty, perhaps even a beauty, but she was in the city now, and everything had changed. Madalena could see that the girl felt as if her features had coarsened, and her build become somehow agricultural, and a part of her wanted to rush over and say, *Me too*.

Mauro seemed to sense her worries, and he would give her hand a squeeze, or pull her close. She hoped this was his way of showing her that his feelings hadn't changed, that he still loved her, and that to him she was still the most beautiful girl in the world.

★   ★   ★

One day they met up after a morning of looking for part-time jobs. Madalena had been recruited straight away to work on Saturdays at a pharmacy counter, and Mauro was confident that one of the opticians he had approached would take him on to file their contact lenses and keep the displays free of fingerprints. As they sat on the edge of the fountain in the park and exchanged notes about their day, Madalena noticed an exceptionally well-dressed middle-aged woman approaching.

She sat beside them. 'I'm sorry to interrupt,' she said, then she introduced herself and explained that she ran a modelling agency, and had noticed Mauro from the other side of the park. She told them she would like to arrange for him to have a session with a photographer, to see if he looked as good in front of the camera as he did in the flesh, and to find out whether he had the potential to be a model. She said she couldn't promise anything, but if the shoot went well he would probably get quite a lot of work. She handed him her card and asked him to have a think about it, and to call her if he was interested. Apologising again for interrupting, she said goodbye to both of them and walked away.

'She seemed nice,' said Madalena.

Mauro shrugged. 'Most people are nice,' he said, putting the card in his pocket. 'Come on.' He took her hands and pulled her to her feet. They walked around the park, and didn't mention the woman again.

Two weeks later he received his first modelling cheque.

He had never had so much money, and he announced to Madalena that he was going to spend it on a romantic night in a five star hotel. Madalena drank her complimentary champagne, made the most of her fluffy robe, ordered their evening meal from room service, and wallowed in the soft sheets of the enormous four-poster bed as he told her how easy it had been, and how he already had more work booked in so they could afford to spoil themselves this once. As they lay together Mauro kissed her, and told her that he loved her, and all the time she kept reminding herself to smile, to see this good fortune as *theirs*.

The next day they checked out of the hotel with moments to spare, and settled back into their old routine. That night Madalena lay in Mauro's bed, and looked at his face as he slept. She tried to see if he had become even more beautiful since coming to the city. Nothing had changed. He was just the same as he had always been, and she found herself wishing he wasn't quite so handsome, his smile not so dazzling, his hair not so thick and his skin not so flawless. She felt a pain in her belly. Eventually she slept, and when she woke the next day it was still there, a constant dull ache.

Within weeks he was everywhere: smouldering down from billboards, smiling on the front of breakfast cereal boxes, and stripped to the waist on the covers of magazines. When life-size cardboard cut-outs of him started being stolen from clothes shops by teenage girls, the story made the television news and suddenly everybody knew who he was: *Mauro*.

It became hard for him to move around the city without attracting attention. He tried wearing dark glasses and a cap pulled down over his eyes, but it rarely worked. Wherever they went groups of girls would approach, asking to have their photographs taken with him. As Madalena discreetly moved out of the shot the girl with the camera would sometimes ask her if she could take the picture so they could all be in it. They spoke to her as if that must surely be her job: they could see no other reason for someone like her to be hanging around with Mauro. Often one or other of these girls would write something on a scrap of paper and slip it into his back pocket.

When it was finally over and they had gone, giggling and waving, on their way, he would squeeze Madalena's shoulder, and give her a smile that said *I'm sorry about all that*, before emptying the contents of his back pockets into a litter bin without even looking at the phone numbers, the love hearts and the dirty invitations scrawled in lip liner.

He started being paid to appear at parties to celebrate the launches of motorbikes, watches, hotels and colognes. He would be paraded around by somebody from the company, and introduced to all the people who mattered. His agent told him to act as if he was there because he wanted to be, not because he was being paid, and to give the impression that meeting all these new people was a real pleasure. She also said that it would help if he could exude an air of availability. He didn't know how to go about exuding an air of availability, but it didn't seem to matter because he always ended up surrounded by women twirling their hair around their fingers, long nails poking from the glossy coils. He kept an eye on the clock, and as soon as his contracted time ran out he excused himself and slipped away, to meet Madalena and tell her how stupid it had all been, and talk about how useful the money would be when the time came for them to set up their businesses and buy a house. She agreed that it was taking them closer to the dream they had been nurturing since their childhoods.

After the launch of a range of luxury glassware they sat together on a bench in a tucked-away corner of the cathedral square. Mauro had been given a set of elaborate sherry glasses in a presentation case. He passed one of them to Madalena. 'Feel how light it is,' he said. 'That was the small talk I was making today, about the delicacy of their design, and the incredible craftsmanship that's gone into them. So don't go saying I have an easy job.'

Madalena agreed that it was very light. She felt that if she held it too tight it would shatter in her grip. Part of her wanted to do it, to squeeze it until it splintered, to feel it turn to shards and powder. She didn't, though. She held it gently, then put it back in its velvet-lined box.

'I've been asked to advertise eggs,' he said.

'Are you going to do it?'

He nodded. 'I think so. After all, I like eggs. The shoot's for five days next week. In the Caribbean. They want me eating a boiled egg on a beach. With my top off.'

'Sounds nice.'

He shrugged. 'It's work. I was thinking about asking them if I could take you, but really it'll just be a lot of hanging around. You would probably find it boring.'

'I couldn't have gone anyway – I couldn't miss that many classes. What about you?'

Mauro looked away. 'I've . . . I've told my tutor I'm leaving. Well, not leaving exactly. I'm going to take a year out, then go back. I can't do both at the same time, and all this is too good an opportunity to miss. I mean, it'll help us in the long run.'

She knew he would never go back. She looked at his face. She knew it so well. What had been the most beautiful face in her town had become the most beautiful face in the city, and the country, and now it seemed as if it was the most beautiful face in the world. People were asking him to cross oceans to look into a camera. And with it right there before her, she could see how fragile this beauty was. Just like the glass, it could be ruined in a moment.

He pulled her close, took her chin between his thumb and forefinger, kissed her, and said, 'You have quite big eyes.'

At the same moment, in a small town in the mountains, a pen could be heard through a bedroom door as it scratched on paper. A poem was being written. The poet knew it could never be sent to its subject, that it would be added to the pile of poems that could never be sent. In this one the beauty of a girl's eyes was praised to the heavens. They were compared with the eyes of other girls from the town, and then with the eyes of the girls in the city, because the poet had been to the city and had seen the girls there, and not one of them had ignited so much as a spark in his heart. In his final stanza he acknowledged that his love would never come to anything, that the girl would always be beyond his reach, but that his devotion would never waver.

Wondering whether anyone before him had used the words *National Bread, Cake and Pastry Expo* in a poem, he put down his pen, sighed, and turned off the light. It was market day in the morning, and it wouldn't be long before he had to start getting the ovens ready.

While Mauro was in the Caribbean, Madalena went for coffee with some of the other girls on her course. She enjoyed talking to them until the subject of Mauro came up. They spoke of how perfect he was, and of all the filthy things they would like to do with him. She said nothing. She didn't want to tell them that she was his lover. There was no way they would believe her, and they would pity her, thinking her a fantasist. Even if she could find a way of proving it to them they would only be baffled, and wonder why on earth he had picked her when he could have chosen any woman on earth.

She excused herself, and as she walked back to her room she passed a vent at the side of a supermarket, and smelled a waft of baking bread. The last thing she wanted to do was think fondly of the sad-eyed boy from her home town, but she had assured him that she would, and she didn't want to break her promise. She stood still, and breathed in. The sound of the euphonium rang in her mind, and though she tried hard to hope that he was getting over her, she knew he never would. She noticed that the smell was nowhere near as sweet as the one that came from his family's bakery. She had found that in the city all the bread was somehow dull, even the freshest loaf seeming as if it had already spent a day or two in the cupboard. She walked on, getting ready to spend the evening alone.

With girls appearing from around every corner, Mauro and Madalena could no longer go to their favourite places without being pestered, so they sought out the more expensive bars and restaurants, where people were supposedly too blasé to pay attention to famous people. Even so, they kept peering in Mauro's direction over the tops of their cocktail menus.

On his return from the Caribbean they met up in the depths of a fancy hotel, in a bar that still seemed tasteful and discreet in spite of its chandeliers and its white grand piano. Mauro let slip that he had a few prints from the shoot with him, and Madalena asked to see them. He was reluctant to hand them over at first, but he relented and passed her a folder. She pulled out the first photograph. He was lying on a sun bed, wearing only a pair of black, expensive-looking swimming trunks while a beautiful young blonde in a tiny golden bikini draped herself across him, feeding him a boiled egg with an elaborate spoon. He told her they had tried it with a fried egg too but it hadn't worked quite as well. It took a moment for Madalena to realise he was joking. He saw the way she was looking so intently at the pictures. 'Her name is Eliska,' he said. 'She's very professional. She has a fiancé.'

Madalena nodded, and looked at the next picture. She didn't know what to say, and was glad when a waiter came over, but as they ordered the same again she noticed a woman coming in who was even more beautiful than the girl in the golden bikini. She felt surrounded. The woman sat at a table on the other side of the room, and as the waiter turned to go Mauro looked over and saw her. Just for a moment their eyes met, and Madalena was caught in the surge of electricity.

Their drinks arrived, and she listened quietly as he told her further tales of egg eating in the Caribbean until she could stand it no longer.

'Go to her,' she said.

'What do you mean?'

'Go to her. You know who I'm talking about. You belong with someone like her, not with someone like me. She's beautiful, Mauro. You two will be so happy together.'

He reached out and gave her shoulder a squeeze. 'I'm not looking for anybody else. I have you. Listen, just because I have this new job it doesn't mean I don't love you any more. That's all it is – a job. Quite a stupid job, too.' It was the first time either of them had ever mentioned that there had been a change between them.

'But Mauro, don't you see? It's not your job that's the problem. This has all been a mistake. We were right for each other in our town because we didn't know any better, but it just doesn't make sense any more. Look at us. Yes, you were the most handsome boy in the town and I was the prettiest girl. But we're in the city now, and you're still the best-looking boy around and I'm . . . well, look at me. I'm ordinary.'

He smiled. 'You're not ordinary at all. How can you say that? You're really . . . pleasant-looking.'

She didn't say anything.

'We made a vow, Madalena.'

'Is that why you're staying with me? Because when you were fourteen years old you made a promise?'

He didn't know what to say.

'We were children, Mauro. We thought things would never change between us, but they *have* changed. I know you would never say so, you're too kind for that, and I know you would never abandon me, but I want you to know that I've thought about it – I've thought about it a lot, and it's OK. I'm letting you go. Go to her, before it's too late. Tell her I'm your cousin, or something like that.'

Mauro shook his head. He reached below the table and gently stroked her fingers with his thumb. 'Madalena,' he said, looking deep into her eyes, 'listen to me: you are the most wonderful person I have ever known.' With a final squeeze of her hand he stood up and walked over to the woman.

Madalena could hear every word. 'My cousin said I would be crazy not to introduce myself,' he said. 'My name is Mauro.'

'I know your name,' she said, smiling and extending her hand, her nails long and red, sharp ends to her soft, slender fingers.

As Madalena passed their table on her way out the woman flashed her a conspiratorial smile, as if to say, *Thank you, Mauro's cousin – I owe you one.*

Mauro didn't notice her leave.

Madalena made her way through the corridors. A man in a cap and gloves held the door open as she went into the street. She had no idea what to do or where to go, so she just walked and walked, following routes she knew, revisiting the places she and Mauro would go before the madness had begun. She stood alone on bridges and walked along the back streets, which without him by her side seemed not romantic but menacing. She hurried to find a street that was busy and well-lit, and when she found one she heard a band playing in a bar, and went inside. Sitting alone with a glass of beer she let the songs take over her emotions. It was a show aimed at tourists who had read about the incomparable melancholy of fado music in their guidebooks, and felt they should experience it while they were in the country. It was all the old songs beautifully sung to a half-empty room, and as she thought of what she had done the words crept under her skin, and she began to cry. There were no sobs, just tears which she let run unhindered, falling from her face onto her clothes.

Other members of the audience noticed her with a sense of satisfaction. *I can't understand a word*, they thought to themselves, *but if it's got that local girl crying her eyes out then it must be the real thing.*

X

In Room Ten, *Count Your Blessings*, a tall, thin boy of nineteen was huddling behind a large display board, listening as echoing voices, some sombre and some emotional, spoke of the sadness of a skeleton. He wished they would stop, and go away.

When the museum first opened, Room Ten had been called *Worse Things Happen at Sea*. Designed to help visitors put their problems into perspective, it had told various tales of human misfortune. Along with the accounts of sinking ships was a series of photographs of a village lost to a mudslide, only its skewed rooftops visible above the new ground level, then there had been a short video presentation about a city decimated by a cloud of toxic gas, and an interactive timeline of global pandemics. Pavarotti's wife had been pleased

143

with this room, but as time went by she started to worry that it might not lift everybody's spirits in the way she had intended, that some people might think it just a little on the negative side. After many sleepless nights she had decided to dismantle it and approach the same territory from a more positive angle, one that was in no way open to misinterpretation. This room being one of the smaller spaces the required upheaval would not be too great, so the old man had allowed this plan to go ahead.

The room was now lined with cork panels, and on a table in the middle were felt pens of different colours, and a pile of blank rectangular cards. On a large display board was an invitation, in several languages, for each visitor to write something good about their life and pin it on the wall so others could be reminded of the good things in their own lives. Pavarotti's wife had gone first, with her card that said *I have four wonderful daughters*, and Hulda had been next, pinning up *The trials of my middle-to-late childhood are over now*. A lot of visitors had joined in, and there were notes that read *I treasure the love of my family; I can see; Ice skating is my passion, and I often find opportunities to enjoy it; I have many valued friends;* and the single word *Horses*. Earlier in the day the boy had read these cards, and many more, and found them all to be smug, or hectoring. *I have food, clothes and shelter; I have fantastic legs; I am in relatively good health; My uncle is fun; My apartment has a lovely view of parkland in one direction, and rooftops in the other.* These were other people's blessings, and each one was a kick in his face. Everything that ought to have been good about his life, that should have brought him joy or satisfaction, had been suffocated by the emptiness that would not let him go, and the words on these cards meant nothing to him. He was sick of counting what were supposed to be his blessings.

Some of the cards had been written in languages he didn't know, and he was glad to have been spared from reading them. The old man, though, was able to understand most of these cards, and as he passed the room on his rounds he had noticed that some had not been written in the spirit in which Pavarotti's wife had intended. One, in Bulgarian, said *Hairy spunk bubble*; another, in Spanish, *I am blessed with a big, hard cock*; and another, in Welsh, *Alun caught VD off his sister.* The old man had left them there, not because he wished to support this subversion of the room's intentions, that was a matter of indifference to him, but because taking them down would have been an unnecessary effort.

The voices moved to the lobby, and at last the good-byes came to an end, and were followed by the sound of footsteps going upstairs. The light in his room went off, the footsteps went away, and then, at last, there was quiet. He got out from his hiding place, stood up and stretched his long legs, which had gone to sleep.

★　★　★

For a few days letters on the subject will be written to newspapers. Professionals in the field will offer level-headed perspectives on what had gone on, and there will be emotional and articulate outpourings from people who had lost sons or daughters, siblings or parents, and who were struggling to make sense of what had happened. They will all offer their own ideas about preventing such tragedies, and each one will be heartfelt, each one different, and each somehow the same.

Along with these, a small amount of letters, written by people with no professed connection to the subject matter, will declare the reported upturn of young men ending up this way to be a direct result of the decline of the French Foreign Legion. Historically, they will say, it had been there as a refuge for the desperate and the lost, giving structure to lives that would otherwise have collapsed, but modernisation had rendered it pointless, its decline having become fatal the moment it was announced that in the spirit of equal opportunities women must be allowed to enlist. They will acknowledge that this ruling had yet to be tested, and for the time being the Foreign Legion remained all male, but the damage had already been done. Such men would no longer be inclined to join up, knowing that at any moment a button could be pressed in Brussels and this edict would be implemented. A charabanc would arrive at the barracks, bringing the first batch of new recruits. The men would be bombarded with reminders of what they had been trying to escape as the garrison filled with pretty girls topping up their tans, tying each other's hair in elaborate plaits, fanning themselves with fashion magazines and doodling love hearts on scented paper. A glimpse of dainty fingers, or a gentle chime of laughter tinkling through the desert heat would, in an instant, render their escape pointless.

Had these incandescent correspondents seen the boy in the museum they would have been obliged to admit that their theory did not apply to him. His limbs were skinny and flaccid, eel-like as he moved awkwardly around the room: women or no women, army life would never have been an option for him. He would have been laughed out of the recruiting office.

The boy's heart raced. He walked around the table, then out into the corridor and through the other rooms, reaching out and running his fingers along the exhibits as he went: dioramas, dummies, latex models of Gadarene swine. He knew that touching exhibits in museums was forbidden, but he didn't care. He found himself excited by the possibility that an alarm would go off, that his next step might trigger it. He waved his arms around, wondering if there was a sensor. Nothing happened. Everything was still again, and quiet. He knew there was somebody else in the building; he had heard them walk upstairs. They could appear at any moment, and the thought made his heart beat faster still. He kept on going, from room to room.

He pressed the light button on his watch, and was surprised by how much time had passed. He had been expecting everything to be over by now, and he supposed he should get on with it. But first he would walk around just a little more. He went into Room Seven, and there before him, its whiteness making it seem luminous in the darkness, was the skeleton they had all been talking about. He stared at it. Then he reached out with both hands, and gently held the skull, and looked into the holes where its eyes had been.

Every once in a while an independent foundation with deep pockets will fund a team of scientific researchers. To give credence to their findings, the scientists they choose will often be Swedish. The instant the money hits the Swedes' bank accounts, instead of vanishing into their laboratory they head straight for the Mediterranean, where they spend their days sunbathing, snorkelling and racing jet skis up and down the coast, dark glasses wrapped around their tanned faces as their fair hair flutters behind them. In the evenings they go out dancing, or stay in and mix extravagant cocktails, throwing their heads back in laughter as they drink them in hot tubs on the roofs of their rented villas. At no point do they spend so much as a moment on research. After a year or two, when the money is running low, they contact the foundation and tell them their study is nearing its end. With heavy hearts they return to Stockholm and, having waited a few weeks for their tans to fade, they hire a conference room and don slightly ill-fitting business wear. The press is summoned, and the scientists sit in a row as their announcement is made.

'We have discovered,' their spokesperson will say, 'over the course of our research, that, in the night-time, the average person will, in their life, eat . . .' Here they leave a pause, building the suspense. '. . . one thousand, nine hundred and seventy-seven spiders.' They would have reached this number by deciding, over calamari and lager the night before leaving for home, that an average of somewhere around one a fortnight sounded about right. With their findings presented, they bid the press farewell, and the item is sent on newswires around the world.

Because only the very brave or the very foolish would ever dare to challenge a Swedish scientist, it is reported as an incontrovertible fact. The sponsors of the independent foundation, usually a manufacturer of mouthwash, will be happy with the outcome of their scientific patronage, knowing that for some time to come people will be a little more inclined to take care with their oral hygiene. Having booked a global advertising campaign to coincide with the announcement, they sit back and watch their sales rise by a small but significant percentage.

Had these scientists done their research, and had they chosen to observe the old man, they would have noticed an unexpected pattern, one which, because they were scientists, they would have discounted as a coincidence. They would not have seen any connection between what was happening in the rooms below, and the spiders that crawled into the old man's mouth.

The old man had noticed this pattern, and having seen an elbow protruding from behind the display board in Room Ten as he had made his way upstairs, he had an idea that a spider would be near.

When he woke in the night, though, it was not the spider's touch that stirred him, but the slam of the fire exit door, and a whoop of what sounded like joy. The old man closed his eyes and began to go back to sleep. This happened from time to time: somebody would change their mind.

He was relieved that he would not have to wake up early for the second day in a row.

The spider scuttled back to where it had come from. The old man's breathing slowed, and the rattle returned. In and out, in and out. It all sounded the same.

PART THREE

I

The first people to be identified will be those who had been reported missing, and whose trails had ended in the city with a final phone call, postmark or cash withdrawal. A photograph from the doctor's collection will be matched with one already in the police files, and for a few days name after name will be released to the press. And then things will slow down.

Having looked forward to months of frenzied coverage, news editors will be disappointed as the story, thwarted on several fronts, stalls much sooner than they had hoped. Early on they will be disheartened by the balanced reactions of the families – instead of the emotional outbursts they had anticipated, their statements will be simple and quiet. Where they had hoped to find condemnation they will find resignation. What anger there is, at the doctor and at those who have gone, will be kept inside. Sometimes there will be an expression of relief at finally knowing what had become of a son or a daughter, a mother or a father, or a few words of self-reproach from somebody who feels they could have done more to help, and there will be sincere, though fruitless, attempts to convey the emptiness left by the knowledge that somebody who ought to have been there, and whose return had been longed for, has gone for ever. There will even be words of pity for the doctor, and sadness for him having turned out this way. In news terms, none of this will propel the story forwards.

The next difficulty for the editors will be its scale, or rather its lack of scale. The early front page cries of *One Hundred Dead in House of Horrors?* will turn out to have been optimistic. Finding that the shards of bone and scraps of clothing correspond with the evidence in the doctor's extensive diaries and painstakingly filed photograph albums, the police will announce the official tally to be a little over a quarter of that. The initial glee at adding a new name to the list of notorious German cannibals will soon fade, leaving them unsure in which direction they should take the story. While it was clear to everybody that the old man and the doctor ought to have behaved differently, there was no reason to believe that in their final moments these people had been victims of anybody but themselves. The faces that look out of the pages of the newspapers had belonged to people who had made their own choices.

And then the stories behind the faces will begin to emerge, tangling things further still. Most will be heart-breaking: the young woman who had seemed so happy with her life and had given no sign of even the slightest turmoil in her mind; the man who had been unable to recover from the loss of his wife; the woman who had been suffering from an agonising and incurable illness. But then there will be the sex attacker, the fraud-ster, the serial bigamist and others who make it seem as if the old man and the doctor had provided a useful service to help rid the world of unsavoury characters.

As announcements from the investigation become fewer and farther between, the editors will be glad of the opportunity to relegate the story to the inside pages. With no serial killer to vilify and no trial to look forward to it will soon fade away, returning only occa-sionally, in ever-decreasing column inches, whenever a batch of evidence slots together and a new identification is announced.

Months into the investigation such an item will appear. Most people will pay it very little attention, but around the world, in cities where the streets are lined with rails and cables, from Changchun to Helsinki, from Sofia to San Francisco, a thousand lonely boys will be unable to look away. They will read the words over and over again, and stare at the accom-panying picture until it is locked in their memory.

She is slightly out of focus, as if her image had been cropped from the back row of a group photograph, and her dark eyes are looking away to the side. Her hair, brown and straight, falls a little past her shoulders, and her lips are parted, revealing slightly crooked teeth. They had never been to her city, but even so the thousand boys feel they have seen her before, at night in an almost-empty tramcar, and as they stare at the photograph it is as if they can hear the soft whirr and clunk of wheels on rails, and the glide of a pole against an overhead power line.

In every language in which it is reported the article will be just a few sentences long, a repetition or slight reworking of the information released by the police. Her name had been Élodie Laroche, she had lived in Lyon, and she was thought to have been nineteen or twenty years old at the time of her disappearance. Her childhood had seen her drift from one foster home to the next, and in her mid teens she had left school without qualifications, after which it was thought that she had started living with men, moving from job to job and from one short relationship to the next.

She had not been reported missing, and had it not been for a dogged landlord's pursuit of a missed rent payment the connection might never have been made. The police had released this information and the photograph, the only recent one they could find, in the hope that they would be able to track down a relative, somebody to whom they could pass on what little of hers they had recovered – a scarf, a copper bracelet and not quite enough bone fragments to fill a shoebox.

The thousand boys cannot understand why nobody had wanted her. They close their eyes, and in their minds they have conversations with her lovers, these Jean-Pierres and Fabrices, Azizes and Jean-Lucs, who recall her fondly enough, saying things like, *She was slim, and I like that*, but when asked why they had let her go, they shrug. *She was a bit strange, I suppose. A bit quiet.*

Did you love her? the boys ask.

The men almost laugh, and shake their heads. *No,* they say, *it was only ever a casual thing.*

The boys picture the final scenes of these brief affairs: the man telling Élodie that he needs some time alone, and Élodie silently packing her belongings into a single case and walking through the streets, getting on the first tram she sees and riding up and down the line, wondering what she will do this time, where she will go. It gets so late that the tram stops running, and she has no choice but to get off. Once again she finds herself unpacking her case in a small room near a terminus, and finding a job in a café or a cheap hotel, where she will meet somebody who, for a while, will let her into his life.

The thousand boys are overcome by an urge to track these men down and put them in headlocks until they explain why they had not taken better care of her, but as they rise to their feet they realise that these Jean-Pierres and Fabrices, Azizes and Jean-Lucs are not to blame: the fault lies instead with boys just like them, boys who would have sat across from her in almost-empty tramcars late at night. Mute and inept, they would have listed reason after reason why they couldn't approach her:

> She probably has a boyfriend.
> I don't think that spot has quite gone away.
> I shouldn't have eaten onions earlier.
> My hair looks fluffy today.
> She wouldn't like me anyway.

As they carried on adding items to this list they would reach their stop and go away, and they would never see her again. They had let her drift into the arms and beds of men too stupid to realise what they had.

The thousand boys close their eyes again, and other details from her life appear before them – the unknown father, the alcoholic mother, the siblings she had never met, the disappointment in the eyes of the foster parents as they wished they hadn't been assigned such a withdrawn child, and the girls who had made her every schoolday a misery. They will see how easily somebody just like them could have reached out to her, and made things better, but they had let the opportunity pass. They feel the weight of responsibility, but at the same time they feel something they had never felt before. They feel ready.

They put the newspaper away and return to their lives, knowing it won't be long before they fall in love with a sad-eyed girl in a tramcar, and that this time they will not just sit there making excuses to themselves. The next day they see her, and when she looks up and their eyes meet, they smile.

Instead of returning this smile, the girl turns her head in a way that makes it clear the attention had not been welcome. They wait for the familiar burn of humiliation, but it doesn't come. Instead they realise their judgement had been clouded by impatience; the girl's sadness had been nowhere near as deep as Élodie's, and was probably no more than the mild and transient melancholy that follows a dull day at work. They wait for the next pair of unhappy eyes, and if necessary the next, and sooner or later it happens.

On trams around the world the girl will look back at the boy, and for a fraction of a second her eyes will return his smile, and he will say something to her, and sit beside her, and she will start talking too, and they will lose track of where they are, riding around the city until the sound of metal on metal stops and they get out and look up and down a dark street, with no idea which way to go.

Wearing an exceptionally comfortable pair of pyjamas, Doctor Ernst Fröhlicher was lying in bed. When he had finished reading his latest medical journal, he wrote his daily diary entry, then he opened his bedside drawer and took out a small pile of pieces of paper torn from newspapers and magazines, each one carrying a charity appeal. One by one he went through them, and one by one he wrote cheques proportionate to how sad each plea made him feel. By the time he was finished he had planted several trees, bought a well for an African village, funded eye operations for a dozen Indians and housed a dog. When all the envelopes were addressed and sealed he took some time to relax, flipping through a large album of photographs of all the bodies he had received from the museum. He looked at the overweight man, who had been such a struggle to lift but who had seen him through a whole winter. Then came the woman with the unbearable line of dark fuzz above her upper lip, and on the next page, lying on the garage floor with her eyes closed, was the girl he had kissed.

As he had laid her out, stripped her and sponged her down, he had been unable to stop himself from wanting her. He had leaned in towards her, and waited for Ute to appear, to glare at him and make him stop, but no vision came, and gently he kissed the girl's lips, which, despite being still and cold, had an irresistible softness to them. He knew at once that he had to feel this softness again, and he moved in for another kiss. This time he parted her lips with his tongue, and felt her slightly crooked teeth. With his mouth still pressed against hers, his breath trembling, he ran his fingers through her hair, then he squeezed her small breasts and licked her belly, and trying hard not to think about what he was doing, he mounted her, all the time whispering words of love.

When it was over he wept, and told himself again and again that he was *not like that*, that he had only tried it once to see what it was like, and besides he had been so lonely and he had thought that it would be like being back with Ute. But it hadn't been. He finished cleaning her up, and put her in the freezer.

From then on he tried his best to treat her body as he would any other. He made no mention of this episode in his diaries, and whenever the memory reared up before him he told himself he had made a mistake, that was all, and he was *not like that*. He ate her more hurriedly than usual, and for once he was not transported by the meat. Instead of the delicious taste that he had come to expect, it seemed to have no flavour, and to be difficult to chew and swallow, and not once did it take him to a world without pain. With every mouthful came a reminder of what he had done, and Ute's continuing absence was more damning than any appearance would have been. *She meant nothing to me, Ute*, he said out loud, as he stuffed the meat in his mouth. He wished he could tell her that he hadn't even known her name, but he had done. He had seen it in her passport. It had been a French passport, and he had burned it until there had been nothing left but a pile of ash, which he had hoed into a flower-bed.

Over the following weeks, knowing it was wrong to waste food, he hurried to finish her and his patients shook their heads, and said to one another, *I do hope Doctor Fröhlicher is taking care of himself. He appears to be gaining weight.* It was around this time that he bought a bicycle, and since then, on dry days, he would ride it to work.

He closed the album, and looked at the ceiling. He hoped Ute would understand, and forgive him.

A thousand babies will be born, each one a girl, and when the parents have the conversation about what to call her, the fathers will suggest Élodie.

Why Élodie?

I just like the name. I think it sounds nice.

Although it is unusual in Zagreb and Odessa, and in Melbourne, Buenos Aires and Alexandria, the mothers will nod. *Yes,* they will say, *it does sound nice.*

II

Pavarotti's wife had engaged a press cuttings service to look through newspapers and magazines for mentions of the museum, and their findings were sent directly to the old man. The first item to arrive had been a feature about short breaks in the city. The article opened with rapturous descriptions of the castle, the river, the shops and the galleries, and went on to devote a short paragraph to the museum, calling it *incoherent and insensitive*, and saying that at points it came across as *a handy advice shop for the emotionally fragile*. The old man thought this to be quite a reasonable appraisal, but he knew that if Pavarotti's wife was to read it she would decide that sweeping and tiresome changes would have to be made. With his long, grey fingers he rolled the clipping into a ball, and threw it into the bin.

The next mention had also been buried within a larger piece. This time, though, it had been broadly positive, so at the start of the next meeting he had handed it over to the proprietor, whose eyes widened as she stood up to read it aloud. '*This unusual museum,*' she said, '*should be commended for bravely confronting a difficult topic.*' That week she didn't propose any changes.

The old man wasn't always able to intercept bad news. Towards the end of one meeting Pavarotti's wife, who had seemed agitated throughout, held up a copy of an English language guidebook she had found in a shop. Her face was white as she opened it at a marked page and stood up. She cleared her throat, and in heavily accented English she read. The author began innocuously enough, writing that it was an unusual way to spend a rainy half hour, and suggesting that the more psychologically robust reader might like to give it a try, particularly as admission was free and its toilets were kept nice and clean. Her voice got higher and higher in pitch and volume, building into an almost operatic crescendo as she read the concluding sentence: '*A curious mixture of stark, disturbing realism and high camp.*'

'My English is quite proficient,' she said, catching her breath, 'but I was unfamiliar with the phrase *high camp*. I made an enquiry, and I have been informed that this expression means . . .' She sat down, and fanned herself with a folder. '. . . it means *extreme homosexuality.*'

Pavarotti looked at the floor, and the old man said nothing.

'Herr Schmidt, as our resident linguist, can you tell me if this translation is correct?'

The old man wasn't at all interested in entering a conversation about the nuances of the term, so he nodded.

'I just don't understand it,' she said, shaking her head. 'It must be a mistake. I shall ask for a correction to be made for the next edition, but for the time being I am afraid you must be prepared for people to come here expecting to find something quite, quite different.' With another sigh, and a shake of her head, she looked at her notes for the final topic to be discussed: *Visits from parties of schoolchildren.*

The old man loathed the idea of parties of school-children parading through the museum, but he wasn't worried. At a carefully chosen point he would stamp on the idea, citing health and safety regulations. He gave the impression of listening intently, but he could see the shape of the cake tin as it pressed against the canvas of her enormous bag, and could think of nothing but what was inside. After a while her tone changed, and he could tell she was coming to the end of the subject. He tuned back in.

'The earlier we reach people,' she was saying, 'the greater chance we have of pulling them back from the brink.'

She had spoken before about how she was convinced

that everybody has within them the potential to end their own life. She believed that most people were fortunate enough never to know of this possibility, that their circumstances kept them from coming close to staring into the darkness. Others, though, would not be so blessed. Whenever she watched children at play she felt her chest tighten at the knowledge that every one of them contained a spark of this awful possibility. She looked at their faces for signs, but they only ever played as children do, running and shouting, jumping and climbing, unaware of their capacity for dread and despair. She wondered whether she should be less concerned about the more serious-looking children on the peripheries of these scenes, the ones who already seemed to have an idea that the world could be a cruel place; maybe they would be more ready to absorb the blows that life threw at them. She knew there was no way of truly knowing which of them were most at risk, and her plan was to get as many children as she could through the doors of the museum. If ever any one of them was to find themselves desolate and in need of hope, it would rise in their memory as both a beacon of light and a warning of what a terrible mistake they would be making.

Since her own childhood Pavarotti's wife's thoughts had often returned to the ever-present possibility of despair. She knew that like everybody else from her birthplace she was one step closer than most people to slipping into a state of misery. For Pavarotti's wife had not always lived in the city: for the first thirty years of her life she had lived in a town in which the inhabitants had no choice but to face the horrors of the world.

She had lived in Hamelin.

There is a certain kind of historian who is never happier than when offering prosaic explanations of tales that have entered into legend. They devote year after year to sucking the life from some of the oldest, most beloved stories ever told, doing all they can to turn the extra-ordinary into the ordinary. With hollow glee they announce that their research has proved beyond doubt that there was no King Arthur, or that while William Tell had existed he had missed the apple and shot his son's ear off, or that Robin Hood was French, and had lived not in the forest but in a charming village in Provence, where he had neither robbed from the rich nor given to the poor, and had been on perfectly cordial terms with the local magistrate. Many of these historians turn their gaze to the story of the Pied Piper of Hamelin, and when each new explanation emerges a fresh round of bickering begins as they do all they can to tear one another's theories to shreds. Some are adamant that the children lost to the town had died of the plague, while others say they had been killed in a landslide, or had drowned in the river, or been slain on a children's crusade. No matter how far-fetched their own theory, at no point will any of them countenance the possibility that a disgruntled rat-catcher in brightly coloured clothing might have charmed the children with the music of his pipes, and led them away to their doom.

There is one thing, though, that these historians do agree on, namely that something awful had really happened, and that many young lives had been lost. Year after year they quarrel among themselves, but the town has long since stopped listening.

For the most part the people of Hamelin spare little thought for the story that surrounds them, but they can never completely escape it. Sometimes as they go about their business they freeze, thunderstruck by the realisation that if these children hadn't died then people would never even have heard of their town, let alone visited in their thousands, spending money and bringing prosperity to generation after generation. In sharp focus they see themselves and their neighbours as insects crawling over a mound of tiny corpses, sucking what they can from the sweet, decaying flesh. In these moments they know that the story is not history. In lands that are not very far away, even in their own land, children are suffering because the world they have been born into is not fair. But they know they will continue to grab more than their fair share because they are unable to care quite enough about people they will never meet. They can see with absolute clarity that the story lives on within every one of them.

Soon this feeling subsides and they feel embarrassed, and remind themselves that they are just ordinary people leading ordinary lives, but these moments of revelation are never far away. It is clear to everybody who encounters them that the people of Hamelin are different from others. Even those, like Pavarotti's wife, who have left the town behind them still carry these feelings wherever they go. Often people will remark that they look a shade paler than they ought to, as if they have come face to face with something they should never have seen.

While most of the people of Hamelin are able to keep the lost children in the background of their lives, there are those who find it impossible, who are unable to rid themselves of the image of them being so happy one minute, their little hands clapping and their little tongues chattering, and so frightened and confused the next, unable to understand what is happening to them. Feeling a constant need to know that they are honouring their memory, these people do whatever they can to harness the sadness of the story and the crushing guilt it has inspired, and turn it into something positive.

For years Pavarotti's wife had tried to work out what she should do. The charity opera galas had been a start, but they had always left her with a sense that she could be doing more, and it was only when she was struck by the idea for the museum that she knew she had found what she had been searching for. At last she was making amends, one lost soul at a time.

III

The old man's wife had never asked him for money, and he was under no obligation to give her any, but every month half his wages went from his bank account to hers. This way he could not be accused of having treated her unfairly, and his days would not be complicated by formal arrangements, or letters from lawyers. From the remainder of his wages he bought cheese, crackers and laundry powder, and sometimes a new set of clothes or a dictionary, and the rest he put aside, saving for the day when he could afford to walk out of the museum and never return. To bring this closer, he took extra pay in lieu of days off.

He planned to go in the middle of a shift, leaving the door wide open and taking nothing with him but a small case containing only a change of clothes and a few essential papers, and walking to the railway station and getting on a train to a town far away. It will not matter which town, it will only matter that it is far away. Arriving at nightfall, he will find lodgings with an old woman, the kind who will mind her own business, and he will lie down in his blacked-out attic room and sleep, and stare into the darkness, and think of nothing. Once a week the old woman will leave a slab of cheese, a large packet of crackers and some fresh laundry outside his door. She will know that she is otherwise to leave him alone.

Shortly after her husband's name appears in the newspapers the old man's wife will be tracked down by a reporter. Quite prepared for the knock at the door, she will invite him in and talk openly and at some length about her married life. This will be the only interview she is prepared to give, and she will take care to be thorough.

The reporter will be able to tell that she is answering his questions honestly and comprehensively, but even so he will be dismayed by how little he learns about the man. He will have been hoping to hear of an underlying problem that might have triggered his unusual behaviour: a domineering mother perhaps, or crippling erection difficulties. Nothing so helpful will be mentioned, and the little that he does learn will serve only to accentuate the man's elusiveness. In the resulting article, titled *A Hunger Too Deep*, he will find himself focusing on the doctor, and in spite of the exclusive interview the old man will remain a cold, blank presence. He will find himself padding things out with an interminable passage about sanity, insanity and culpability, and a lengthy summary of cannibalistic activity in Germany through the ages, as if the old man and the doctor had been participants in a rich national tradition. Although he will make a reasonable amount of money from his work, he will be disappointed with it.

Towards the end of their conversation, the old man's wife will open a drawer and take out a small bundle of photographs of her husband in his younger days, and in every one he will be sporting an extraordinary moustache. The reporter will be unable to disguise his admiration, and she will acknowledge that she too cannot help but be impressed by the sight of it, even after her abandonment, and the passage of so many years, and having come to learn of the events in which he had been involved. She will say that it had seemed to be the only thing he had ever truly cared about, and once it was gone there was nothing.

Ever since he had seen a photograph of Kaiser Wilhelm II, it had been his ambition to match his iconic moustache. It had begun as an irregular spread of thin, wispy hair, but soon the down coarsened into bristle, and darkened, and he was able to trim, wax and sculpt it into the style he had been working towards. By the time he considered it finished it was grand, and wide, and its tips were upturned as if defying gravity. It attracted many congratulatory comments, but what nobody mentioned was that for all its perfection it seemed somewhat incongruous on the otherwise smooth face of a twelve-year-old boy.

While the boy's face and body changed, the moustache remained the same, and it accompanied him through his studies at university and into his working life, and it was there on the day he married the quiet daughter of his next door neighbour. He had thought that a conventional union would help ease his passage through life, and, to an extent, it did. He no longer had to think about his laundry, and meals would appear before him at their allotted time, but there had also been sighs, and tears, and marital obligations to swiftly and silently fulfil. It soon became clear that he had made a mistake, and without a word of explanation he moved into the spare room.

He had always known that one day the moustache would enter a decline, and that when it did it would have to go. As he entered middle age and its black bristles no longer matched his hair, which had turned quite grey, he decided that the time had come to take a razor to it, and in a few minutes his life's work was gone.

The stranger in the mirror looked back at him in disgust. He could see straight away that this had not been the time, and he immediately started waiting for the bristles to return. When they did they seemed defiant, as if exacting their revenge on him for having doubted them. No matter how sternly he coaxed them, the moment he thought he had returned the moustache to its former glory a stray strand would jump out of place, rendering the overall effect commendable, perhaps even outstanding, but never quite exemplary. It made people think of Edward Elgar, or Umberto I of Italy, sometimes even Le Pétomane, but never of the Kaiser. For months he tried to live with this impostor but one morning, defeated, he shaved it off again, this time for good, and as he stared into the eyes in the mirror he understood that in a moment when judgement is clouded it is possible to make a mistake that can never be put right.

His wife watched him leave for work, and when he got home that evening he found her in the hall, surrounded by trunks. In her hand was a framed photograph from the early days of their marriage. 'I think there was a time when I loved you,' she whispered. 'I think there was a time.'

'Unpack your belongings,' he said. 'I shall be the one to leave.' It was the longest conversation they had had for some time, and he never saw her or spoke to her again. After a single visit to a lawyer, in which he transferred everything they had shared into her name, he left town with only a thin bundle of banknotes in his pocket. He wrote a short letter to the laboratory, telling them he would not be returning, and offering no contact details.

Days later he started at the Koblenz and District Museum of Food Hygiene, where his job involved standing still, staring straight ahead, and very occasionally gesturing in the direction of the toilets.

The old man sat behind his desk, staring straight ahead. It had been half an hour since Hulda had gone, smiling, into the morning, but the museum had yet to receive a visitor. He sensed somebody coming in, and knew at once that she was there not to look at the exhibits, but to find him. They always knew where to find him.

The clack of heels stopped in front of his desk, and he looked up. He had not seen this one before. She was young, slim and smartly dressed. She leaned across the desk, lifted a small digital recorder to his ear and pressed *play*. He listened, and when the recording ended he wrote the name of a Silesian village on a piece of paper. She picked this up, and dropped an envelope in its place. She walked away, and with his long, grey fingers he slid the envelope towards himself, and put it in his inside pocket. The entrance hall was still and silent again. He stared straight ahead.

After this intrusion the day continued like any other. A few visitors came and went, some of them leaving with grave faces, shaking their heads and mumbling to one another that *It really makes you think*, while others tried to stifle giggles as they rushed past him and out of the door. But in the early afternoon he received a second unexpected personal caller.

'Good afternoon, Herr Schmidt,' said his visitor, smiling.

The old man said nothing. He waited for the doctor to continue.

With the museum dark and empty below him, the old man sat at his kitchen table. He reached into his jacket pocket, took out the envelope that the woman had delivered and opened it. As usual it contained some banknotes and a handwritten, unsigned letter. He counted the money, and unfolded the letter. He read that with his last accent identification he had been instrumental in the capture of the serial child abductor Erwin Krebs, previously known as the Wild Boar of Brunsbüttel. The recognition of a half-Flemish parent had been the breakthrough they needed. *Without your talent and cooperation the Wild Boar would have had the opportunity to strike again, and once more we find ourselves thanking you.* With his long, grey fingers he rolled the letter into a ball, and put it in his mouth.

As the paper soaked up the light trickle of saliva, and slowly turned to pulp, he thought back to the doctor's curious monologue. It was the first time they had met outside their early morning encounters, but the doctor had addressed him as if they were on familiar terms, first complimenting the museum, then expressing concern at the old man's pallor and suggesting some dietary improvements, particularly at breakfast time, but it had not been long before he arrived at the real reason he had driven over on his lunch hour. He explained that he was approaching his final body, and that it would be a terrible shame if he was to run out altogether. 'After all,' he said, 'I am sure you wouldn't want me going hungry in the wintertime.'

He said this as if the old man had known all along about his eating habits. He hadn't though, and he looked at the doctor for an indication that this was a joke. None came.

In idle moments the old man had supposed that the corpses were used for either sexual gratification or medical experimentation, but it seemed he had been mistaken all along. It was neither here nor there to him what the doctor did with them, but he was irritated with him for having made explicit something that until that point had been unspoken: that each of them knew the other's behaviour to be irregular. His visitor had carried on, telling him how useful it would be if he was to help things along just a little, that if the opportunity was to arise then perhaps he could *assist a poor soul with their decision-making*, and *assume the role of counsellor by tipping any balances that might need to be tipped*. He illustrated this tipping with a lengthy hand gesture.

'I am sure you agree that for medical reasons it is best for such people to avoid prolonging their distress, and what you would be doing is providing them with a framework within which they are able to exercise their free will. I'm sure you are aware that this kind of thing is very fashionable in Switzerland, but in our case we needn't concern ourselves with all the cumbersome bureaucracy.' The old man said nothing, and the doctor continued. 'I know I can rely on you. After all, friends help one another out.'

The old man bridled at this. All his life he had gone out of his way to avoid any situation that might be mistaken for a friendship.

The doctor carried on. 'As much as I would love to stay here and chat all afternoon I have to get back to my clinic. All those ill people won't be able to cure themselves.' With a wave, he left the museum.

The old man's annoyance had clung to him for the rest of the afternoon. The doctor had clearly been in an agitated state, and he didn't want him losing control and doing something that would lead to them being found out. If Pavarotti's wife was ever to hear about what had been going on she would be sure to close the place down. For the first time he hoped the museum he was working in stayed open. He was close to having enough money to retire, and he wanted to stay where he was for the remainder of his working life. His duties were light and he was well-paid, and he didn't want the upheaval of moving to a new job in a new town, but more than anything he didn't want to lose his supply of cake until the very last moments of his museum career.

He found himself becoming angry at the thought that the doctor might throw all this into jeopardy, and he supposed that on balance the course of action that would cause him the least potential upheaval would be to do as he had been asked, to tip any balances that might need to be tipped. He would only be assisting in natural selection after all, and as always when there was a death in the building there would be no need to feel any sorrier for the person involved than he would for an unlucky sperm. Once again he reminded himself that his hands would remain clean: all he would be doing is cooperating with a medical professional.

There hadn't been a body for some time, but he knew it wouldn't be long before somebody was to come in with dark rings around their eyes, and shoulders slumped in defeat. When this happened he would do what he could to make sure they didn't run, whooping, from the back door, but were carried out and bundled into the doctor's car.

He swallowed the last of the paper, took off his shoes and polished them to an impeccable shine. When this was done he washed his hands and sat back down, staring straight ahead and seeing nothing, and thinking nothing, but all the time waiting, as a spider waits for a fly.

IV

Mauro didn't stay with the girl from the hotel bar. Nor did he stay with the Taiwanese model from the jeans commercial, the golden-haired singer from the music video or the pristine older woman who had discovered him in the park. Lovers came and went through the enormous doors of his penthouse apartment, but Madalena was sure a time would come when one of them would stop him in his tracks. She could see that he was really just biding his time until he found the one he would settle down with, and when that happened all this would be behind him.

A few days after she let him go they had met up and had a long conversation about how they would still be friends – best friends.

'It had just run its course,' she said.

Mauro agreed. 'We'll be like brother and sister.'

She could tell how much it meant to him for them to remain close, and she gathered all her strength. 'Yes,' she smiled. 'Like brother and sister.'

They had made a point of meeting every week. Mauro would embrace her, and start telling her what he had been doing since they had last seen each other. This usually involved things like wearing sunglasses on a yacht, or hanging upside-down from a cable car with an insanely expensive watch on his wrist. Once this was out of the way he would ask her what she had been up to, and even though she didn't do much besides keep up with her studies and her part-time job he would listen intently and take a real interest. Sometimes she wondered if he was clinging to a part of himself that he didn't want to let go, worried that if he lost his rapport with her then the boy from the small town in the hills would be gone for ever, but she always ended up conceding that it was probably nothing as dramatic as this; it was more likely that he just wanted to hear what his best friend had been up to.

After the split they had agreed that they would both be absolutely fine about the other one seeing new people, that there would never be a need to keep things secret. Mauro had honoured this, and always made sure he kept her up to date with the women in his life. Madalena, though, had told him she was at a point where she was happy to be alone, to live her life without having to consider anybody else. He was glad she felt so comfortable this way, but he still hoped she would find somebody. He was sure that one day she would be ready to yield a little of her treasured independence, and that when it happened he would be the first to know.

One night, as they sat on his roof terrace, he brought out a glossy men's magazine. He opened it at a marked double page, and showed it to her. There was no picture, just white lettering on a black background. She read the heading, *LUCIANA,* and the accompanying paragraph:

> Sometimes in Brazil the gene pool flows in such a way that the best of every lineage comes to the fore, and the mix creates not so much a mongrel as a brand new pedigree. Often there's a solid base of Portuguese, a touch of Native American, maybe a north European grandparent or two – add a dash of Lebanese, a pinch of African and a soupçon of Japanese to this heady mix, and you get something quite special. Many of these girls will, fortunately for us, become models, using their natural talents to delight gentlemen the world over. But time marches ever onwards, and now we must concede that the Brazilian beauties we have known and loved have been left standing. The bar has been raised higher than we had ever thought possible – what we

had once thought to be perfection now seems
almost humdrum. Take a deep breath, then turn
the page to see a vision that will burn into your
retinas for the rest of your life.

Madalena took a deep breath, and turned the page.
There she was: Luciana. The prose, which she had
thought melodramatic to the point of hysteria, now
seemed sober and restrained. She was, by a very long
way, the most beautiful woman she had ever seen.

'Meet my new girlfriend,' said Mauro. 'And this time
I know I've found the one.'

Luciana was dressed in very short shorts, and a
tight top that revealed her navel and a glimpse of
cleavage that was almost modest for this kind of
magazine. Madalena looked at the perfect body, and
the unbelievable face. The eyes in the photograph
seemed to gaze back at hers not with the coldness she
had been anticipating, but with warmth, even friend-
liness. She turned the page and there she was again,
this time apparently naked beneath a black silk sheet,
her lips shiny and one sleek leg showing.

'Oh,' said Madalena. 'I think she looks . . . lovely.
Very pretty. Congratulations.'

'Thanks. She's based here at the moment, so we're
seeing a lot of each other. I can't wait for you to meet
her.'

Madalena did her best to smile. 'I can't wait to meet
her too.'

As soon as she finished her coffee she got up to leave, saying she had a lot of studying to do. Mauro handed her the magazine. 'Take it,' he said. 'I don't need it – I've got the real thing.'

She thanked him, and put it in her bag. They walked over to his private elevator, and as he held her tight he had never seemed so far from reach. She realised she had been fooling herself all this time, that what she had thought were feelings of hopelessness had been no such thing. She had told herself over and over again that he was lost to her for ever and there was nothing she could do about it, but now she realised that deep down she must have been hoping he would tire of the endless parade of flawless skin, slender thighs and tight waists, and realise he had lost the most precious thing in his life. But now Luciana was here, and she could tell he meant every word he said. She had never seen his eyes shine this way, not even when they had been children. She felt stupid for having held on to hope for this long, and for having hidden it from herself so completely. From the moment she let him go, Mauro was always going to find the most beautiful woman in the world, and she should have realised this straight away and accepted it, instead of burying herself beneath layer after layer of delusion. Through the haze that surrounded her she realised he was talking to her about plans for the following week, when he would introduce her to Luciana.

'See you then,' a voice said. Her voice. She smiled, and it hurt, as if somebody had grabbed her lips and was forcing them into an unnatural shape. She stepped into the elevator, and the moment the door slid shut, the smile vanished, and her shoulders slumped in defeat.

If only I wasn't such an idiot, she thought, pressing her face into her pillow and willing the students in adjoining rooms not to hear her sobs. *If only I had kept my mouth shut instead of letting him go. He would have been loyal to me for ever.* He would have been too, she knew it. That night in the hotel bar all she had been hoping for were some words of reassurance, but she had sent him away and now he was lost to her. He would never have abandoned her, or cheated on her, or knowingly hurt her, and he would have loved her just enough to be happy. Of course he would have noticed other girls but he would have let them flit past like butterflies, bright flashes of colour that dazzle for a moment before going away, leaving everything just as it had been before. Not knowing what else she could do, she packed her bag, ready for the morning.

When her alarm went off she couldn't be sure whether or not she had slept. Some of the thoughts that had run through her mind had seemed like nightmares, and she hoped they had been, that they were beyond her control. She went to the bus station, trying to convince herself that if she went back to the hills for a few days things wouldn't seem so bad.

★　　★　　★

The young baker's great-great-great-grandmother was up even earlier than usual. She appeared before him as he prepared the day's first batch of bread. 'It's over,' she said.

The young baker was quite accustomed to having no idea what the old lady was on about. 'What's over?'

'That girl you've had your eye on, the beautiful one. She's no longer with her handsome boyfriend.'

Though he had never spoken to anyone but Madalena about his love for her, everybody knew about it, and had grown to accept it as just another part of the townscape. 'I know that,' he said, getting on with his work. 'They broke up a while ago.' Such news was bound to make its way back to the hills, but along with everybody else he was sure this was just a bump on the road, that they would one day reunite. Nobody who had watched them grow up together could imagine their love story having a different ending, and he had not taken the news seriously.

'Well, yes, we all knew that, but now she has given up hope of a reconciliation.'

He put down his bag of flour. 'But great-great-great-grandmother, how can you know?'

'She's back for a visit. Last night, just after you stopped playing that horn of yours, we old people stood in a huddle and silently watched her as she got off the bus. Her cheeks were sunken, and her eyes surrounded by dark rings, and she walked with a defeated slouch. I know she looked much the same the last time she was here, but I can see that since then a part of her has died. You don't get to my age without being able to tell things like that.' She was a hundred and six years old.

The young baker didn't know what to say. For a fraction of a second he felt something like a landslide in his heart, and it revealed a sensation he had never known before. He realised at once what it was. All those years he had been telling himself that Madalena would forever be beyond his reach, but now he knew that somewhere inside he had been wishing that one day something would change, and she would love him just as much as he loved her. For the first time he allowed himself to feel the hope that had always been there.

'I suppose you'll be wanting to take some time away from the oven so you can go around town and *accidentally* bump into her, won't you?'

He nodded. As his great-great-great-grandmother qualified her encouragement by waving her stick and offering thunderous words of caution, he took off his apron and hat, and went upstairs to shower away the smell of dough, and to change into his best clothes.

His customers had all heard from their own old people about Madalena's return, about the dark rings around her eyes and her defeated slouch, and when they opened the door and saw the young baker instead of the usual delivery boy they knew at once what was going on. He joked about his father having demoted him for insolence, but it was obvious why he had taken on the delivery rounds, and why he was so smartly dressed. The quality of bread dipped just a little as the rest of his family manned the ovens, but everybody understood, and nobody complained.

All day he ran errands, his heart pounding as he braced himself for the moment Madalena came into view. She never did. By the middle of the afternoon his deliveries were over, and he began to worry that she would catch the bus back to the city before he had a chance to talk to her. Feeling as if his whole life had been building up to this moment, he gathered his courage and knocked on her door. Her father invited him in. He knew as well as anyone what the young baker felt in his heart, and he thought it would do his daughter good to be reminded that there were other men out there, and that at least one of them thought the world of her.

He sat at the kitchen table, and waited. He heard muffled voices, then nothing. He looked at the clock, and watched the minutes pass. Then, with no warning footsteps, the door opened and she was there. He began to stand up to greet her, but he only got halfway. She didn't look at him as she walked over to the kitchen table and sat down.

'Hello, Madalena,' he said, easing himself back into the seat.

She looked down at her clasped hands. 'This has to stop,' she said. 'You have to forget me. I'm not what you think I am.'

'What do you mean?'

'I mean . . .' She sighed, and after a while she carried on, quietly. 'I mean, I'm not a great beauty, and there's no cause for you to feel the way you do about me. Trust me, I'm nothing special. One day you should go to the city and see for yourself what real beauty is.'

'I've been to the city,' he said. 'I've been there three times for the National Bread, Cake and Pastry Expo, and you're wrong. I know there are girls there with longer legs than yours, with more lustrous hair, and with smaller waists and more delicate noses, but not one of them is as beautiful as you. None of those girls made me forget you, not even for a moment.'

She carried on looking at her hands. She wished with all her heart that it had been Mauro saying this, not this poor boy she hardly knew. The only words she could think to say seemed to be at once inadequate and overwrought, but they would have to do. She knew she had to at least try to stop him from loving her. Still looking down, she said, 'I can't see past my broken heart.'

'Maybe one day you will.'

She shook her head. 'Tell me, is there anything on earth that could cause your love for me to die?'

He shook his head. 'No.'

'Really? There's nothing?'

'No.'

'Then you understand.'

He understood completely. As he looked at her

dark-ringed, down-turned eyes, and her slumped shoulders, the declarations and promises he had prepared caught in his throat. There was nothing more to say, but knowing he mustn't run away, or just sit there saying nothing, he asked her how her course was going.

Without looking up she told him her marks had been high, but that she was going to have some catching up to do when she got back. Quietly, she asked him how his baking was coming along. He told her it was going very well, that business was good, that he was taking on more and more responsibilities, and his father was getting ready to make him an equal partner in the company. She asked him how his great-great-great-grandmother was filling her days when she wasn't standing in a huddle and silently watching people getting on and off the bus. He started to tell a story about her, imitating her voice with uncanny accuracy as she banged her stick and delivered her prophecies. At last Madalena lifted her eyes, and looked at him as he spoke. He was mimicking her toothless expression, and for the first time in days she smiled. Immediately she felt crushed with sadness that she could never, not even for a moment, return the love of this pleasant, funny and talented boy. By the time he finished the story she was looking at her hands again, her shoulders slumped.

'Believe me,' she said, 'I'm not what you think I am. It's not just the waist and the nose and all that. There are other things. Things I can't talk about.' She didn't want to tell him, or anyone, about the thoughts that had been running through her mind, thoughts so ugly that she knew they made her unworthy of anybody's love.

'You can talk to me about anything,' he said. He wondered whether he should tell her some bits and pieces about himself, about his box of poems, or how sometimes after work he would climb to the mountaintop and look out at the horizon and imagine how wonderful his life would be if she loved him in return. But he knew he didn't have to, that all this would have been as clear to her as it was to everybody else. Instead he smiled, and told her what she already knew. 'My feelings haven't changed since the day I gave you the doughnuts,' he said. He told her he loved her, and that he would always be there for her if she needed him.

She supposed this was her cue to tell him that he was mistaken, that he couldn't possibly love her because he hardly even knew her, but she had learned that things didn't work this way. She had barely known Mauro when she had fallen in love with him. They had been children, just playmates, and then one day the explosion had happened, but she knew her love had been real from the start. Mauro had told her he had loved Luciana the moment she walked into the room, and that she too had loved him as soon as she saw him. His eyes had sparkled as he said this, and she felt no reason to disbelieve him. Madalena was in no doubt that the young baker adored her with all his heart. 'Find somebody else to love,' she said. 'Please.'

He shook his head, and stood up. 'Tell me though, before I go, when you're in the city and you smell baking bread, do you ever think of me?'

She looked up. Her eyes met his, and she nodded. Then she looked back down at her hands and spoke, her voice the faintest whisper. 'Every time.'

'Madalena,' he said, 'I'm going to ask one last favour of you. If you can find it in your heart to do just one thing for me, please could it be this.'

She didn't say anything. She dreaded what he was about to ask of her.

Undeterred, he made his request. 'Madalena, please would you move to an apartment above a bakery.'

He had hoped this would make her laugh, but it hadn't worked. With one last look at the girl he loved, he wished her well, and said goodbye.

The sun went down to the sound of a dented euphonium. Madalena lay on her bed, her eyes closed. She covered her head with a pillow, but it was no use. She could still hear it. It was more beautiful than ever, and more desolate, and she wanted it to stop.

On the bus back to the city her family's voices rang in her head, telling her it was *not the end of the world*, that she had *so many good things in her life* and that *in time this trouble will pass*. They had seen somebody who was going through an awful experience but who was going to get better. She wished she had a way of telling them how she really felt, and of some of the thoughts that had gone through her mind, thoughts that had frightened her, *really* frightened her. After a few hours she supposed she should eat something. Her mother had given her some fruit and a small loaf of bread for the journey. She took the bread from its paper bag, and saw that it had been baked in the shape of a love heart. She broke a piece off and put it in her mouth. It was the best bread she had ever tasted, and before long only crumbs were left, and she brushed them to the floor. She rolled the paper bag into a ball, and put it in her pocket. She looked out of the window. A milestone told her there was still a long way to go.

The day came when she had arranged to meet Mauro and Luciana. She had hardly slept, and she sat at the back of the room as her professor wound up his morning lecture. She hadn't been able to concentrate, and had written only a few lines of notes. She read them back, and they made no sense. She couldn't work out what she was doing there. This course had been part of the dream she had built up with Mauro, with her pharmacy on one side of the street and his optician's shop on the other, but the dream had turned to dust, and she felt she was wasting her time.

The professor told them that in the afternoon they would be going to the laboratory for a lesson about professional standards in the handling of acids, about preventing injuries and dealing with mishaps. She pictured a bottle of liquid as clear as water and as vicious as fire, and she thought of Luciana, and imagined herself taking the bottle and emptying it into that perfect face, right there in the middle of the bar. She pictured her screaming and falling to the ground, her skin a mess of burns and blisters.

This image had flashed through her mind for just a few seconds, and when it was gone she was furious with herself, and ashamed, and frightened of where these thoughts might lead. She tried to concentrate on the professor's voice. With the lecture over he was making jokes, and the people around her were laughing as they packed away their books, but she didn't hear anything amusing in what he was saying. As she closed her bag and stood up, she thought of her next lesson, of the gloves and the goggles, and of a bottle small enough to slip into a pocket and take into the world.

Mauro had introduced Madalena to a lot of his girl-friends. On hearing that their lover's best friend was a girl they smiled just a little too much and felt their nails harden, but as soon as they saw her their worries evaporated. They thought it was lovely that he had kept his friend from the small town he had grown up in, and they started to wonder if they knew any unremarkable but good-hearted boys they could introduce her to.

Luciana's nails had not hardened when she heard

about Madalena, and she had not over-smiled, but like the other girls she liked her as soon as she met her, and started to mentally pair her off with various cousins. Madalena, the dark rings around her eyes disguised by make-up, found the strength to chat quite amiably as if nothing was wrong, but all the time she felt as if rats were eating her from the inside. She had been wondering whether there had been some trick photography used by the magazine, but even dressed in jeans and one of Mauro's shirts Luciana looked as flawless as she had on the page.

Mauro's other girlfriends had been pleasant and polite, but their conversation had consisted of little more than descriptions of the fabulous hotel rooms they had stayed in, and recitations of long lists of luxury brand names and exclusive shops. Luciana, though, seemed to have only a passing interest in the glamour that surrounded her, and at the point of the conversation where the girlfriend would normally be delivering a monologue about her favourite spa treatments, she was instead telling a series of humorous anecdotes about a heronry on her uncle's farm. At one point she even did an impressive impersonation of one of the birds, and Madalena noticed that Mauro was laughing along, not in the *I'm-only-laughing-because-you're-so-pretty* way he had with the other girls, but because he was really finding her amusing. He and Luciana were compatible to the point where it seemed they were the only members of their own extraordinary species, and

Madalena wished she could feel happy that they had found one another. It just wasn't possible though, and while she smiled on cue she hated Luciana more than she had ever hated anybody. She hated her, and she hated her uncle and his fucking herons.

When Mauro left the table to go to the toilet Luciana confided in her as if they had known one another for years. 'I've never been so happy,' she said. 'I always wanted to meet a man like Mauro, but my friends said I never would, that no such man exists. But look,' she gestured towards the empty chair, 'he does.'

As Luciana carried on, Madalena smiled and slipped her hand into her bag. Her fingers ran over the edges of her keys, then moved to the sharp end of her eyebrow tweezers before resting on a small, square bottle. Her thumb slid along the glass until it found the metal cap. The bottle contained only perfume, but she took comfort in the thought that it could have held enough acid to strip the skin from Luciana's face. That afternoon she had held a phial in the laboratory, and been sure she could have taken it away without anybody noticing. She hadn't, though. *Next time*, she thought. And then, with horror, she thought, *No, not next time. Not ever.*

'But enough about us,' said Luciana. 'How about you? My cousin Rui is visiting in a couple of weeks – I think you would like him. We could go out together, the four of us.'

'Oh, thanks, but I'm . . .' She knew she had to kill

this plan as quickly as possible. '. . . I'm already seeing somebody.'

'Hey, that's great,' Luciana's eyes shone with real delight. 'Tell me all about him.'

Madalena felt her life draining from her body, but somehow she found the energy to appear sprightly as she told Luciana all about the boy she was supposedly seeing. For some reason, she had no idea why, she called him João.

When Mauro returned to the table Luciana started telling him about Madalena's João, how they had met at college and been friends for a while, and how they had secretly liked each other for a long time and had been out on three dates, and how it all seemed to be going very well.

'That's fantastic,' said Mauro, thrilled by the news. 'Let's all go out, the four of us.'

Madalena shook her head. 'No,' she said. 'Not yet. It's early days, and I don't want to frighten him. Maybe in a few weeks.'

'Oh, go on,' said Luciana. 'It'll be fun.'

'Well . . . why not?' She was desperate for this assault to end. She had gone bright red, and at last they stopped asking her about this João, believing her blushes to be a symptom of blossoming love. She hated that they were so happy for her. She had never felt so stupid. Now the only person she wanted to throw acid over was herself.

★　★　★

She lay on her bed, and picked up the magazine that Mauro had given her. She turned to a photograph of Luciana. The thought of what she had wanted to do to her made her stomach feel as if it was shrivelling to the size of an artichoke heart. She ran to the sink, and vomited. She hadn't eaten for hours, and spatters of what was left inside burned her throat. She cupped her hands beneath the cold tap and took a drink of water. She rinsed the sink, and tried to tell herself that she would never have gone through with it, that all she had done was cling to the idea that she *could* do it so she wouldn't feel powerless in the face of such perfection. She had no way of knowing if this was true, but she couldn't hide from the knowledge that she had made a detailed plan to disfigure somebody, and that was all she needed to know for sure that she was a horrible person. She covered her face with her hands as it came back to her that she had invented a boyfriend. She had given him a name and a life, when really there was nobody. She was dangerous *and* ridiculous.

She lay back on the bed and opened the magazine, looking from one picture of Luciana to the next, and hating her so much it hurt. When she couldn't stand it any longer she turned to a random page. Here there were no pictures of beautiful women, just an item called *It's a Crazy World!*, a collection of oddments sent in by readers on their travels. One of the items caught her eye. It was a paragraph about a museum in Germany. The magazine seemed to be making fun of the place, but she didn't see what there was to joke about. She wanted to go there. She had to go there. She needed the museum to tell her that the decision she had made was the right one. She had no idea how long it would take to get there, but she started packing a small bag. Once again she set her alarm for early morning. She would make sure she was on the first train out of the city.

V

The certainty of her damnation became too great a burden for Hulda to bear on her own. She was determined, though, that it must not dominate her days, that life must go on in spite of her inevitable destination. She knew she needed to find ways of making sure she never allowed the despair to defeat her, and she decided that the best thing to do would be to approach the wisest-looking member of her congregation and ask for advice. One Sunday not long after her eighteenth birthday, she had caught up with him as they filed out of the church. 'Excuse me, sir,' she said, 'but I wonder if I could talk to you about something.'

'Of course.' He smiled kindly through his large, white beard, and Hulda knew at once that she had found a friend.

They walked a short distance to a small park in the

shadow of the castle, where they sat on a bench. He listened to her story, and when it was over he confirmed that she was beyond all hope of salvation. 'But you are by no means alone,' he said. 'There are more of us than you will ever know.'

'More of *us*?'

He nodded. 'Many years ago I made the same mistake as you, young Hulda. That's right,' he chuckled, 'even I, even old Herr Friedleben, shall be heading downwards when the time comes.' He told her that his circumstances had not been as dramatic as hers, that he had merely been a wayward young man with a loose tongue, who drank and cursed with little thought for the consequences. By the time he realised what he had done it was too late. 'Just as it was for you, the moment the first unforgivable blasphemy passed my lips I was lost.'

Hulda felt awful for him, but she knew he was not inviting pity. 'Maybe I will see you down there,' she said.

He sighed, and shook his head. 'I don't think the Devil will allow us such comforts as glimpses of familiar faces. It's best to be realistic, Hulda: Hell will be an eternity of unremitting agony for both of us.' She nodded sadly, and he took what looked like a business card from his pocket, and began to write. 'I am going to invite you to a meeting. Twice a month a few people with our difficulty have a little get-together. We have all accepted that we have no chance of getting into heaven, but we share a determination not to fall into the trap of living our lives the wrong way. As we lie dying we shall know in our hearts and minds that we have not allowed Satan to be our master until the very last moment. This way we shall leave with a small sense of triumph. These meetings help us to maintain our resolve in the face of temptation and despair, but more importantly than that, they give us a good excuse to eat biscuits.'

He handed over the card, and smiled. 'We are called the Union of the Damned. We don't like to draw attention to ourselves, and I am sure you understand the value of discretion, so please tell nobody.'

Hulda looked at the card. Herr Friedleben had written an address, a date and a time. She turned it over, and on the other side were the words that had become so familiar:

> Whoever blasphemes against the Holy
> Spirit will never be forgiven; he is guilty
> of an eternal sin.   Mark 3:29

'I leave them lying around here and there,' he said. 'You never know, maybe one day somebody will see one and be saved. It's just a little idea of mine.' With the help of his stick, he rose to his feet. 'Please do come along. And remember – bring biscuits.'

Hulda watched him walk away. She thought he was a lovely man. She only wished he wasn't going to Hell.

She knew it was selfish to think this way, but she also wished he had given her better news. Still, the sky was blue. That was something.

Biscuits aside, she had no idea what to expect. She worried that the meeting would be all candles, robes and incantations, but when she arrived at the address on the card she found a very ordinary suburban home. A dozen people were sitting on sofas and dining chairs, making light conversation about any subject but perpetual suffering. Herr Friedleben greeted her warmly, and called the meeting to order.

Each member took a turn to speak. The first admitted that since their last get-together he had fallen prey to thoughts of how unfair it seemed that murderers could be granted forgiveness, while good people who had made a single mistake would remain beyond hope of redemption. He said he had felt angry with God for refusing to accept his heartfelt apologies, and had even come close to repeating his fateful transgression. This was greeted with words of understanding, and Hulda was comforted to find it was a familiar problem. She had fought this anger too, and there had been times when she had felt a sense of injustice at the knowledge that her stepfather, the man who had pushed her into the arms of the Devil, would have the opportunity to make his peace and spend eternity in heaven. The next man to speak told everybody he had been having difficulty sleeping for fear of what awaited him, and she empathised with this as well. Next, an attractive young woman confessed that she had been facing a battle to remain faithful to the Lord. She had been wondering why, when nothing she could do would ever change her destiny, she should not sink into a life of sin. She explained that she had sinned a lot in the past – predominantly fornication – and had found it very enjoyable. 'Every day opportunities arise,' she said, 'often with very handsome men, and sometimes the temptation is almost too much to resist.'

Such opportunities never arose in Hulda's life, but even though she couldn't empathise with the woman's situation she thought it was nice that nobody rushed to condemn her for having had these urges; instead they congratulated her for having been strong enough to keep her resolve.

Hulda's turn came, and for only the second time she told the story of her darkest night. When she was finished she received many kind words, and she smiled at Herr Friedleben, grateful to him for having introduced her to such pleasant people.

After a short biscuit break the mood of the meeting changed, and they began discussing the good things they had done since their last meeting, things which, when the time came, would help them to look the Devil in the eye. One of the men had raised money for charity by running a half marathon, another had accompanied a group of disadvantaged children on a kayaking trip, and the attractive woman received a very warm response to her announcement that she would soon be leaving her bank job to start training as a paramedic. Hulda was very impressed with all these tales of human decency, and for a moment she wondered whether only the damned could be truly good, knowing that there would be no reward beyond the passing satisfaction of having scored a small victory against their future tormentor. She stamped on this thought, knowing she must never consider herself to be in any way superior to people who had not taken the same wrong turning as her.

Not long after this meeting she was offered the job at the museum, and she accepted it without hesitation, delighted to know that she would be playing a small role in an establishment that brought hope and comfort to the wretched. She told her fellow members of the Union of the Damned how thankful she was to them for having guided her in the right direction.

One evening she turned up to find no sign of Herr Friedleben. There was no discussion that meeting, they just sat in quiet contemplation. There were tears and there were sobs, but most of all there were biscuits. The plates kept going around, and they ate and ate and ate. They knew he would have wanted it that way.

For all her participation in these sessions, Hulda never found the right moment to talk about her plan to vanquish the Devil. Night after night, as she waited to fall asleep, she nurtured the idea of marrying, and of having at least two children and raising them, from their very first day, not to do as she had done. Satan would be getting her soul, but if she could provide at least two servants for the Lord, then she will have added to the overall stock of good in the world, and as her life slips away she will know that for all her wailing and gnashing of teeth, she had been the true victor. What she needed to set this plan in motion was to find somebody to love, and who loved her in return. Her thoughts kept returning to Pavarotti, and the possibility of him having a brother who was like him in every way. She hoped that one day she would find the courage to ask.

In the meantime she would keep on smiling.

VI

When the finer points of the doctor's activities are revealed, only one person from his life will be prepared to speak out in his defence. In a long letter to a newspaper, Ute's mother will write that anybody who had truly known her daughter would understand how this poor man had come to lose his mind. She will beg all those who are condemning him to transfer the blame to her own shoulders, saying that the moment the child was pulled from a slit in her belly and dangled before her she had known that she would leave only misery in her wake. The dread only intensified with time, but her love for her daughter was so overwhelming it had left her weak, helpless even, and she had not known what she could do except hope that one day the girl would stop being the way she was. She will go on to say that she should have heeded her misgivings and stopped the wedding, or after the funeral she should have stayed in contact with the doctor, maybe even marrying him herself so she could monitor him and make sure his suffering was not manifesting itself in destructive ways. She should have done *something*, then all this would never have happened. But it *had* happened, and she will finish by declaring that she wishes with all her heart that she had wrestled the child from the midwife's hands, and dashed her brains out on the hospital wall.

The trainee who opens this letter will assume it had been written by a crank, and put it in the *no* pile.

Doctor Fröhlicher was eking things out. He was nearing the end of his penultimate body, and had less meat than usual on his plate. He wondered whether in going to the museum he had crossed a line. As he ate on, he reassured himself that he needn't worry, that with his good work, his charitable donations, his ethical shopping choices and his decision to bequeath all his possessions to the poor, he had built up so much moral credit that he could afford to allow his behaviour to drift into a grey area every once in a while. And besides, he told himself, this area was only a very pale grey; all he had done was suggest that the old man might wish to encourage people to end their lives in the comfort of the museum rather than else-where. As a place to spend final moments it was certainly preferable to a bridge, or a garage, or a railway line, and he supposed this was why it was such a popular spot. These were unhappy people whose minds were already made up; if they were to lose courage and carry on living they would only continue to be unhappy. The old man would be doing them a favour by helping them to leave their misery behind sooner rather than later.

'Of course,' he said, 'it is a terrible shame that these people do what they do, but they will have exhausted every other avenue, and it is helpful for all concerned when they do it in the museum. This way they have not died in vain. You see, Hans, if our supply was to dry up, who knows how downhearted it would make me? Maybe I would even become too despondent to cure people.' He threw a small fatty chunk in the air, and the dog leapt up and caught it. 'If you look at it that way, these poor souls are just like you and I – servants of Hippocrates.'

The doctor was feeling more optimistic than he had for a long time. With the nights drawing in, and people's thoughts turning ever darker, he was sure it wouldn't be long before somebody was to arrive at the museum in search of release from their troubles. And in the meantime he had a whole body waiting for him.

When his plate was clean he went through to the garage and opened the freezer. There it was, naked and ready, crystals of ice brilliant white against the skin. The doctor had eaten a Vietnamese woman before, and a Turkish man, but this would be his first taste of such dark brown, almost black, flesh. He felt a little embarrassed about having been so wary of it, and for the last time he reminded himself that he was a doctor, that his training and experience told him the flavour would be much the same as if it had been any other colour. 'Even at very low temperatures,' he called through to Hans, who had stayed in the kitchen, 'food cannot be frozen indefinitely.' It was time to get on with it. He assembled his equipment and started getting the body ready.

By the time the job was finished the man was in pieces: some parts were defrosting on trays in the refrigerator, and others were hanging from hooks. A few bits had been set aside for Hans, and anything unsalvageable had been thrown into a black plastic sack. The doctor swabbed the floor, and all that was left to do was clean himself up and change into a fresh pair of pyjamas, then he would be able to unwind in bed with a glass of water and a leaf through one of his photograph albums.

As he turned off the light he saw that a small red indicator was shining from the empty freezer where the body had lain curled up for such a long time. He walked over to the socket on the wall and was about to pull out the plug when he stopped. He decided to leave it on. He had a feeling it wouldn't be empty for long. Somewhere somebody would be on their way.

PART FOUR

I

By the time the sun came up and she could see out of the window, Madalena's train had left the city and was passing through countryside. She felt numb. Then she felt sick. Then came a raging pain, as if insects were trapped inside her body and struggling to scrape their way out through her skin. One by one these insects gave up, and she felt numb again. She hoped this would last, but soon the nausea returned, and the scraping. Her eyeballs throbbed.

The train slowed to a halt. She had taken the first one going in the right direction, and it seemed to be stopping at every station along the way. There would be three changes before she reached her destination. It was going to be a long journey. She looked up to see that somebody had sat down in the seat across from hers. She knew she mustn't draw attention to herself, that she had to get there without anybody finding out what was happening to her.

She closed her eyes and pretended to sleep.

II

Not far from Doctor Fröhlicher's house was a large park where people would go to walk their dogs. Often the doctor would take Hans there, and for a while he would merge with his surroundings, the complications of his life ebbing away as he became just another man taking a stroll with his dog.

In the clear light of the Sunday morning he stood on the path in his coat and scarf, and watched Hans run across the grass, his paws marking green tracks through the frost as he hurried to play with a familiar Afghan hound. For a few minutes he lost himself in the serenity of the scene, happy just to watch his dog. His heart sank as he heard a pair of feet scrape to a halt beside him. He knew what this meant: one of his patients had seen him, and had decided to pass the time with a little light conversation. As always this conversation would begin with some mild observations about the weather and the glossiness of Hans' coat, followed by some words of admiration for *men of medicine*. Then, lost for what to say next, the patient would start making small talk about anything medical that entered their mind. He reminded himself that this was one of the hazards of the job. On his first day at medical college he and his fellow students had been taught that everybody feels the need to make polite conversation with doctors, but very few people know how to go about it, and once the civilities are over they flounder. Before they were taught anything about healing the sick they learned a number of techniques for coping with the tedium of such encounters. Remembering his training, he readied himself for this familiar ordeal. He turned in the direction of the sound, and it was just as he had supposed: his patient Irmgard Klopstock was smiling up at him, her short, grey hair peeping out from her woolly hat. He returned her smile.

'Good morning, Doctor Fröhlicher,' she said, her voice quavering, as if it was on the edge of nervous laughter.

'Good morning, Frau Klopstock.'

'It's very cold today – the first really cold day of the year.'

Doctor Fröhlicher nodded, and returned his gaze to Hans. Together they watched him play.

'Hans is such a lovely dog. And what a glossy coat he has – you must feed him only the finest food.'

The doctor acknowledged this with a smile and a nod.

'I hope you don't mind me saying, doctor, but it is so reassuring to see you relaxing. You deserve it. I have nothing but admiration for you men of medicine. You all work so hard.'

'Thank you,' he said, impatient for her to continue her walk so he could go back to unwinding, 'but it's just a job like any other.'

'No, no, you are being modest. You work very hard.'

Although obliged to deny it with a shake of his head, he agreed with her. Doctors did indeed work exceptionally hard, and he knew he worked harder than most. Since Ute died he had only ever taken three days off each year, one on her birthday, one on their wedding anniversary and one on the date of her death, and only then if they fell on weekdays.

'You are tireless,' she said.

'As a matter of fact, Frau Klopstock,' he said, 'I am rather tired at the moment.' It was true. With so much on his mind he had been having difficulty sleeping, and he hoped she would take the hint and carry on with her walk.

Frau Klopstock mistook the comment for a joke. 'Oh, Doctor Fröhlicher, I have always admired your sunny way. I shall never forget your wonderful bedside manner when I had that problem with my . . .'

She stopped, and Doctor Fröhlicher carried on looking at Hans.

'Oh, I'm being silly. You are, after all, a man of medicine. There's no need for me to be bashful with you . . . when I had that problem with my anus, Doctor Fröhlicher, and you were so patient with me. You went out of your way to put me at my ease.'

The doctor recalled the problem. He had indeed been patient with her, but he was always especially patient with people who came to him with such troubles. Every doctor has an area of particular interest, and this area interested him greatly, so much so that the probing and the observations could almost count as a hobby. He would take investigatory photographs which, strictly speaking, did not need to be taken, and which, once taken, ought really to have remained among confidential files; they really shouldn't have found their way into a series of albums that he kept on top of his wardrobe, and which he would sometimes leaf through last thing at night. He smiled at the memory of Frau Klopstock's difficulty, and told himself that at some point over the weekend he would make himself a mug of hot chocolate and have another look at the pictures.

'And then there was the time I had that terrible pain in my shoulder. It just wouldn't go away, and, doctor, I came to you . . .' And thus continued a full summary of her recent medical history. With the highlight over so early, the remainder was quite unexceptional. There were aches, rashes, viruses and a toe that was not broken after all, just badly bruised. The only moment of drama came when she recounted the difficulty she and her husband Franz had experienced in their attempts to conceive a child. Marrying late in life they had known it was likely to be difficult, but, as she explained, it was still very saddening to find that it was a biological impossibility. When her exhaustive account of his prescription of a mild topical fungicide for an easily combated skin complaint ended with a sigh, it was clear that she had finished, and Doctor Fröhlicher supposed he should say something.

'But you are well now?'

'Oh yes, doctor. Although I have lately been suffering from an occasional very slight toothache.'

'I suggest you see your dentist about that.'

'Oh, of course. I was just mentioning it, since you asked. After all, I'm sure you're interested in medical difficulties no matter where they occur in the body, aren't you, doctor? Oh look, here comes Hans.'

The Afghan hound had been called away, and the Labrador ran up to his master and rubbed against his legs.

'It has been very nice talking to you, Frau Klopstock,' said the doctor, 'but we really must be off now.' He put Hans on his lead, and began to walk away. After a few paces Hans stopped, and began to choke. Nothing came up. The doctor could feel Frau Klopstock's eyes following them, and he knew it wouldn't be long before she said something.

'Poor Hans,' she said, as she glided towards them.

'He will be fine. I expect he has just been eating twigs or fallen leaves.' Doctor Fröhlicher patted Hans' rump, and they made it a few more paces before the dog started to choke again. This time whatever it was that had been bothering him came up and lay on the ground, steaming in the cold air. Doctor Fröhlicher led Hans along, but they had only gone a few paces when his patient's voice called from behind.

'Doctor Fröhlicher,' she said.

He turned to see her bent over, staring down at the pile of vomit.

'Oh, Doctor Fröhlicher,' her voice was quavering even more than usual, and her hand was pressed to her heart. 'I think you should come here. Hans does indeed seem to have brought up some leaves and, I think, a very small twig. But it's not only that, doctor – he also seems to have produced something else . . .' She looked up. 'Something rather extraordinary.'

Doctor Fröhlicher walked back towards the scene of Hans' choking fit. And there, in the middle of a puddle of slime, lay a large, dark brown penis.

The doctor had to think fast. 'I am very sorry that Hans has embarrassed you in this way, Frau Klopstock,' he said. 'Please look away.' She closed her eyes and he took a plastic dog-mess bag from his pocket, bent down and picked it up. He tied the bag shut.

'You may open your eyes.' He lowered his voice and moved his head towards hers, emphasising that he was taking her into his confidence. His mind raced as he calculated the best thing to say, and the most doctorly vocabulary to use. 'I am afraid, Frau Klopstock, that what you have just witnessed is something of a hazard of my profession. A general practitioner's dog will often find himself party to very unfortunate, in this case tragic, incidents. And sometimes, in the mayhem of a medical emergency, the innocent hound, knowing no better, will . . . sample a foodstuff that he ought not to have sampled.' He cast his eyes in the direction of the parcel in his hand.

'Oh, Doctor Fröhlicher, I had no idea. How terrible – for you, and of course for the poor soul.'

'I am, as you say, a *man of medicine*. It's all part of a day's work for me. However, you are absolutely correct to observe that this kind of episode is indeed awful. I can assure you, though, that I shall personally reunite this part of the poor man's anatomy with the rest of his remains in good time for his interment.'

She nodded.

'And of course, Frau Klopstock,' he said, 'you will understand that this all-too-commonplace aspect of the job is not one which the profession wishes to advertise. I have no doubt, though, that I can count on your tact in this matter – for the sake of the departed, of course.'

'Doctor Fröhlicher, my lips are sealed. After all, it would be little comfort for the poor man's family to know that this awful incident had occurred – here in a public park, as well. You doctors never cease to amaze me with your dedication and discretion.'

223

'As I said, it is just a job like any other. Now if you will excuse me, Hans and I really must head home. We have something of a busy day ahead.' He put the plastic bag in his coat pocket. 'Come, Hans,' he said, and they walked away.

When they had gone only a few metres Hans stopped, and once again began to retch. Something came out, but Doctor Fröhlicher, impatient to get away, pulled his dog along, not looking to see what had emerged this time. Frau Klopstock, on the other hand, found herself overwhelmed with curiosity and was unable to resist going to see what Hans had brought up. The doctor was stopped once again by the sound of her voice.

'Doctor,' she called. 'Doctor Fröhlicher, your dog has just vomited something that looks to me like a . . . oh dear . . . oh, doctor, I wonder what the medical term is?' She didn't want to appear foolish by using the wrong words. She looked at the wrinkles, and the wire-like hair, and thought back to her Human Biology lessons at school. At last the phrase appeared in her mind, and her eyes lit up. 'Doctor, it appears to be . . .' she put her hand to her mouth. Remembering the importance of discretion, she continued in a stage whisper, '. . . it appears to be a scrotal sac.'

III

After sitting on a station bench for almost two hours, Madalena boarded her second train. As it idled at the platform she took a pen and pad from her bag and started making notes. She wrote that she felt as if she was being attacked by the world and by herself, and as if barbs were tearing at her skin. She read this back and could see how inadequate it was, how it didn't come close to capturing how she really felt. Knowing she had to do better she carried on, writing that she hated herself, that she was an idiot, and a liar, and dangerous. She said she could see no light, that she knew she could never be a worthwhile person, or a happy one. This was more like it, but as she went on it became clear that so many of the feelings that were assaulting her couldn't be pinned down by language: they were unique to her, and there was no reason for anybody to have come up with words for them. There were so many of them too, each one different from the next. She thought for a moment of the eyes of a fly, but flies' eyes were orderly, and her feelings were a mess. To capture and record them she would have to create a whole new lexicon, and that would be pointless because only she would be able to understand it, and anyway most of these feelings didn't give her nearly enough time to evaluate them, they just burst into her life for a moment, spitting their venom before going away to be replaced by something similar in its ferocity but different in every other way.

She carried on, writing simple words that she knew could never fill this vacuum but which she hoped would help the people she loved to know she had been released from something unbearable. She used words that they could at least begin to understand: *pain, darkness, disgust*. On the page they looked melodramatic, and feeble. She wrote that she was more frightened of living than she was of dying. *I am scared*, she wrote, over and over again. She finished with what she knew to be a clear, simple truth: that what she was going to do would be best for everybody.

She looked through what she had written. It read like notes for an awful, attention-seeking teenage poem. She would have to start from scratch later on. She tore the page in half, then half again. She looked out of the window, wondering when the train was going to start moving. A girl of about six was on the platform, standing beside her mother and waving to somebody in the next carriage along. Madalena hated her. The child was beautiful, and she would remain beautiful, and without even knowing it she would spend the rest of her life blithely trampling on the feelings of people who didn't deserve to have their feelings trampled on. The girl's waving was joined by face-pulling and laughing, and Madalena's hatred spun around and savaged her. The little girl was wonderful, a lively, funny, happy little person. The realisation that she was capable of such vicious thoughts about somebody so perfect and so pure made her even more certain that she was doing the right thing.

Two women were sitting opposite her, talking in a language she didn't understand. They had seen her tear the paper. One of them gave her a smile, and took a bunch of bananas from a bag and offered her one. Madalena shook her head, and looked out of the window. At last the train began to move, and the little girl jumped and waved as they rolled away.

The train entered a tunnel, and a face she never wanted to see again looked back at her from the black glass. She closed her eyes, and pretended to sleep.

IV

Irmgard Klopstock sat across the dinner table from her husband, Franz. As usual neither of them spoke, and all that could be heard was the tick of the grandfather clock, the clink of cutlery and the soft slurp of chewing. Franz hadn't noticed that his wife had been in a state of turmoil since returning from her walk in the park, and as far as he knew this silence was as comfortable as ever. All day Irmgard had been agonising over whether or not she should say anything about her unusual encounter with the doctor and his dog. At last she decided that Doctor Fröhlicher, always such a reasonable man, would understand that there must be no secret between husband and wife, no anxious moment left unshared. On the eve of their marriage she and Franz had agreed to confide in each other no matter what situations were to arise, but theirs had been a marriage in which situations had rarely arisen, and it hadn't been often that she had felt the need to confide anything. She braced herself, and began.

'Aren't general practitioners wonderful, Franz?' she said.

Franz carried on chewing his potato salad as he nodded his agreement.

'Of course,' she continued, 'there are all the things we think about straight away – their kindness to the sick, their patience, their dedication to their vocation, the way they put their own health at risk with all those germs flying around . . . But it's not only these obvious things, is it Franz?'

Franz shook his head. 'No,' he said.

'It's not just offering diagnoses, they also have to consider all aspects of hygiene at every moment. And then there's the paperwork – they have to write everything down: the symptoms, the treatment given, any referrals made and so forth. It's imperative that medical records are kept up to date, and it's such a shame that we ordinary people so rarely give any thought to such a central part of their working day.'

Franz nodded again. 'Yes.'

'And when the weekend comes and the final patient has been seen, and the last piece of paper placed in its correct position in the filing system, and they think they can finally unwind by going for a nice stroll in the park, their dog opens its mouth and out comes a human penis. They really are astonishing people, aren't they Franz?'

'Astonishing, Irmgard.' He carried on with his potato salad.

The meal continued, and all that could be heard was the tick of the grandfather clock, the clink of cutlery and the soft slurp of chewing. Then, halfway through dessert, Franz lay down his spoon, sat up straight and looked directly at his wife.

'What was that you said earlier, Irmgard?' he asked. 'Something about . . . a penis?'

With great relief, Irmgard began the story of her walk in the park. She left out no detail, and when she had finished her husband said, 'I agree with you – general practitioners are indeed remarkable people. And it's not only doctors, Irmgard. Let's not forget the nurses and the other staff who work in the medical field, facing horrors every working day. They put industrial packaging managers to shame, even industrial packaging managers who are really rather high in position.'

'Oh, Franz, you mustn't think that way. Your job is important too.'

His mouth downturned, Franz nodded.

Irmgard felt a weight lift from her shoulders. It seemed that even though he had never mentioned it, her husband already knew that this kind of episode was quite commonplace. She marvelled at the lengths to which men will go to shield their women from the darker side of everyday life.

Franz Klopstock liked to wind down after his evening meal by sitting in his favourite armchair and reading a chapter or two of a technical manual. This evening though, his mind kept wandering from the diagrams and data back to his wife's account of her walk in the park. Just before nine o'clock, when Irmgard was upstairs writing a letter to her sister, he put down the manual, picked up the telephone and called Manfred, his cousin-in-law from Wolfenbüttel. Manfred just happened to be a general practitioner with a dog, an affectionate lurcher called Johannes, who brought a smile to the face of everyone he met.

Manfred sounded delighted to hear from his cousin-in-law, and straight away they started talking about the technology behind a proposed series of updates to the water purification process in Mecklenburg-Vorpommern. On Franz and Manfred's first meeting the subject of civic water supply had filled a silence as they stood beside an outdoor tap. Neither of them had had more than a passing interest in the subject, but each knew just about enough to sustain a short conversation. Thinking the other to be wildly keen on the topic, they each went away and made a point of reading relevant items in newspapers so they would have something to talk about at the next family gathering. From then on their conversation almost never strayed from the subject, and over time they found themselves becoming genuinely interested in what they found out, and they began to look forward to their encounters. 'Look at them,' the women would say. 'They always have so much to talk about.'

After half an hour their telephone conversation was still going strong, but Franz knew that the time had come to broach the subject of Irmgard's trip to the park.

'And tell me,' he said, 'how is Johannes?'

Manfred was a little surprised by this uncharacteristic sidestep, but it was a simple question which he had no difficulty answering. 'He is in good health,' he said, 'and as affectionate as ever. He still brings a smile to the face of everyone he meets.' Hoping to steer the conversation back to familiar ground, he added, 'He seems to take to our tap water very well. He laps it up from his bowl with considerable enthusiasm, even more so since our local piping system was updated.'

'That's good to hear,' said Franz. 'I've been wondering about his diet. Does he eat the usual things for a doctor's dog?'

'Oh yes, he eats the usual dog food, primarily a combination of biscuits and tinned meat . . . all washed down with water.'

'And is this diet ever supplemented by . . . oh, you know . . . miscellaneous human body parts, and things like that?'

'Well, no, of course not. We do sometimes feed

him some appropriate leftover food from our plates, but by and large he eats – and drinks – quite conventionally.'

'So he never snacks on, for example, the genitalia of a male corpse?'

'No.'

There was a silence.

'Franz,' said Manfred, his tone grave. 'Is there something you wish to tell me?'

Franz replaced the receiver with a heavy heart. Irmgard was still upstairs writing to her sister, and he took Manfred's advice and dialled his old friend Horst for an informal chat. Horst was a policeman, and though Franz had known him since childhood he had never before had cause to call him in his professional capacity.

'I'm sorry to bother you at this hour,' said Franz, 'but I wonder if I could talk to you about something that has arisen. Something rather unsettling.'

Horst could tell from his friend's voice that this would be best dealt with in person. 'I shall be with you in nine minutes,' he said.

Not long into their courtship, Franz Klopstock had addressed his wife-to-be by a pet name: *Mein kleines Glühwürmchen*. My little glow-worm. She had looked at him as if he had suffered a blow to the head. Feeling compelled to explain himself, he said that he had called her that because his life had been one of darkness until she had come along, bringing with her a beautiful and unexpected light. Her expression hadn't changed, and he carried on, telling her that it had seemed as if he had been walking lost through a forest in the night-time and had suddenly seen a brilliant symbol of hope, a reminder that dawn would arrive, heralding a bright new day.

'Oh,' she said. 'I see.'

She had seemed so taken aback at being addressed in this way that he never used this pet name, or any other, again, but as he stood at the foot of the stairs he knew that this was a time when a gentle term of endearment was required, and it was the only one that came to mind. 'My little glow-worm,' he called, gently, and moments later his wife appeared. She was smiling, but her face betrayed her fear that he would never have used those words unless something serious had been afoot.

'What is it?' she asked, as she made her way down-stairs.

'Horst is coming to visit.'

'How nice,' she said.

'I'm afraid it won't be very nice, my . . . my little glow-worm. He will be visiting us in his capacity as a police officer. I think he will be asking you to tell him what you saw in the park today.'

She turned pale, and put her hand to her mouth. It had been hard enough for her to use those awful words in front of her husband, and she moved her hand to her heart at the thought of going over the same details with somebody else. 'Must I, Franz?'

Franz nodded. 'I'm afraid so. But remember, Horst will be speaking to you not as a friend, but as a police officer. You are not to feel embarrassed by the subject matter.'

'But Franz, you don't think, do you, that . . . that Doctor Fröhlicher has been up to no good?'

'Oh, no. No, no.' He dismissed this notion with a wave of his hand. 'No, no, no. There will be a perfectly reasonable explanation. This time tomorrow we will have forgotten all about the whole episode.'

They moved together into the living room, where they sat in silence, and waited for Horst to arrive.

V

The old man sat at the kitchen table, and stared straight ahead. With a long, grey finger he slid a pamphlet towards himself. Pavarotti's wife had handed it to him at their last meeting, wanting his opinion before deciding whether or not they should add a bundle of them to the rack of similar pamphlets beside the front desk. He unfolded it, and started to read. It was titled *Nature's Life Raft*, and its subject was the antidepressant qualities of serotonin. It explained how leaving some serotonin-enhancing snacks, particularly cashews and bananas, within easy reach of the afflicted could make the difference between life and death. He couldn't understand why people felt the need to interfere with the lives of others, why they had to bother them with fruit and museums, but he would tell Pavarotti's wife what she wanted to hear: that the pamphlet was pertinent, that he believed it must be added to the rack as a matter of urgency, and that it might even save a life.

He went back to staring straight ahead. As much as he believed that people should be left alone, he had accepted that in order to keep the doctor under control there was a likelihood that he would soon be interfering in somebody's decision-making process, and possibly even overriding their free will. This would be an inconvenience, but no more.

For now, though, there was nothing he could do. He had kept a close eye on his visitors that day, and knew he would not be disturbed in the night. Seven people had come in, and seven had left.

The doctor would have to wait.

VI

At Irmgard's request Horst had gone back to his car, and when he returned he was wearing his policeman's cap. She knew that recounting her experience to a friend would have been too much to cope with, but if she could keep telling herself that she was offering information to an official investigation it would be different.

'Thank you, officer,' she said. 'That will be a great help to me.'

The three of them sat at the dining table. Horst sipped Irmgard's home-made gooseberry juice, complimented her on it and listened attentively, taking notes as she gave her account of the walk in the park. When it was over there was a short silence.

'This is interesting,' he said. 'We received a Missing Persons report for somebody of this description some time ago.'

'Somebody . . . of this description?' she asked.

Horst nodded.

'But my description was somewhat specific. Anatomically speaking, I mean.'

'You say the penis was dark brown?'

'Yes.'

'And the scrotal sac was of a comparable colour?'

'It was.'

Horst nodded. 'Well, we must of course maintain an open mind, but for a moment let us proceed on the assumption that the parts you mentioned were from the same body. The disappearance of a gentleman of this very skin tone has been brought to our attention. I wonder . . .' He stroked his chin, and though he looked deep in thought, his mind was blank.

Horst rarely had the opportunity to play detective. His work only ever consisted of simple cases, the kind that other officers would consider distractions, where no arrests or car chases were expected. He often found himself in charge of the Lost Property box, and if there was any traffic to be directed he would always be top of the list. He was also the one who was entrusted with keeping the dustier Missing Persons files up to date, and although he had been marginally involved in some tragic cases, this was the first time that his work had ever involved the mysterious appearance of human body parts. He decided that this was going to be *his* case. He would be the one to get to the bottom of it, even if solving it meant that he would have to break the rules.

His son had always enjoyed telling his friends that his father was a policeman, but the boy was about to enter his teens, and he seemed to be starting to realise that his father's working day did not, after all, consist of him catching dangerous criminals. Horst had been feeling this keenly, and had been looking for an opportunity to make his son proud. This could be it. For the first time in his life he would be a loose cannon, someone who went his own way. He felt his heart speed up.

'But I'm saying too much,' he said. 'We must keep all lines of enquiry open.' He pondered for a moment. 'Tell me,' he said, looking directly at Irmgard. If he was going to crack this case on his own he would need as clear a picture as he could possibly get, and he must not shy away from difficult questions. He was a detective now, and no detective ever got anywhere without digging for the important information. 'This penis . . . how big was it?'

'I . . . I . . .' Irmgard turned even paler, and put her hand to her face.

'I'm sorry to ask you such a question, but you will understand that every detail is crucial in . . .' he tapped his cap with his pen, '. . . a police investigation.'

'Of course.' Irmgard lowered her eyes. 'Of course.'

'So, this object you saw, could you give me an idea of its size?'

As Horst poised his pen on his notebook, Irmgard looked around for something she could compare it to.

Horst helped her along. 'Perhaps in relation to a

comparable part of your husband's anatomy?'

'Oh dear. Well, it appeared to be in a flaccid state but even so it was significantly larger than Franz's even when it is fully erect.'

Horst noted this down, then thought for a while. 'It has struck me that although he is my childhood friend, I have never seen Franz in, as they say, all his glory. Please tell me, is your husband's penis of average size?'

She looked flustered.

Once again he tapped his cap with his pen. 'Every detail is crucial.'

Irmgard composed herself. 'No. From the magazine articles I have read on the subject, I believe my husband's penis to be considerably smaller than average. The one I saw in the park was larger in both length and girth. Substantially larger.'

Franz looked at the carpet, his shoulders hunched.

Horst nodded gravely as he noted all this down. 'And the scrotal sac?'

Irmgard looked at Franz. She felt awful, and was glad of the opportunity to regain some ground for him. 'My husband has exceptionally large testicles, officer.' This was true, and Franz seemed to cheer up a little.

Horst cleared his throat. 'Thank you for that, Frau Klopstock. But how about the scrotal sac in the park?'

'Oh, I see. I am happy to say that from what I could see it was a good deal smaller than my husband's. Maybe of a size that could comfortably accommodate two eggs.'

'Chicken or duck?'

'Chicken. Small chicken.'

Horst wrote the words *small chicken eggs* in his note-book. 'Thank you, Frau Klopstock.' His voice was gentle. He took off his hat, and at last he became Horst the friend again. 'That will be all for now, Irmgard.'

'But Horst, all these questions . . . Doctor Fröhlicher isn't under any suspicion, is he? He has been such a wonderful general practitioner to us over the years. I'll never forget his wonderful manner the time I had a problem with my . . .' She stopped. She had already said more than enough for one day. She quickly thought of another medical difficulty she had suffered. '. . . with my forearm.'

'No, no,' said Horst, smiling. 'No, no.' He told her that she was not to see this so much as an enquiry than as a formality, to set everybody's minds at rest. He said he was certain that the doctor's explanation would turn out to be absolutely mundane, and that all the correct procedures will have been followed at every stage. Guiltily, though, he hoped that there would be some intrigue for him to unearth. 'But I must empha-sise . . .' He put his cap back on. '. . . I must emphasise, for the doctor's sake and everybody else's, the impor-tance of keeping this conversation to yourselves.'

Franz and Irmgard nodded, then Horst's cap came off once again and they walked to the door. Irmgard handed Horst a jar of home-made gooseberry jam, and they exchanged friendly goodbyes.

★　★　★

243

At the end of the street Horst's car turned not towards his home, but towards the police station. He had a hunch that this couldn't wait until the morning.

He knew he would have to work in absolute secrecy. If they found out about this at the station the first thing they would do is sideline him, and pick a squad of younger, fitter officers to investigate the case, leaving him in the cold and without credit. He poured himself a coffee, sat at his desk and got to work. He ran a check on Doctor Fröhlicher. As he had expected, he had never been in the slightest trouble. It was going to be a long night. He called home and told his wife not to wait up for him, and poured himself another coffee. For the first time in his career he undid his top button and put his feet on his desk.

One of his younger, fitter colleagues noticed him. 'Working late tonight, Horst?' he asked.

Horst had his answer ready. 'I'm preparing some materials for a visit to a kindergarten. It's important work. After all, we don't want the kids growing up to be criminals, do we?' The lie sent a surge of pleasure through his body.

The colleague smiled, and went away.

Horst stayed at the station until two in the morning. He checked the Missing Persons files, and saw that the case he had been reminded of remained open. There had been no name or address, only a report of an unpaid bill at a hotel and a copy of an illegible signature in the guest register. The assumption had always been that he had simply left town to save money, but all kinds of possibilities raced around Horst's mind. He had no idea which of these would be worth pursuing, and which would be a waste of time. After a phone call to the local hospital he established that there was no record of anybody having died in recent days who might fit the description Irmgard had given. He could feel that something was not right. He knew that this would not be a case that could be solved from his desk. He made plans for the morning, and headed home.

Still in his shirt and trousers he rolled, exhausted, into bed.

Horst snapped awake at six, pulled on the few clothes he had taken off, brushed his teeth and headed straight out. He knew exactly what he was going to do. He drove to the doctor's house, where he parked a discreet distance away, on the other side of the road.

This was his first stake-out, and his skin prickled with anticipation. Some lights were already on, but for a long time nothing happened. Then the lights went off, and a minute later a bicycle pulled out of the side gate and on to the road, its rider wearing a scarf and gloves.

'The doctor,' Horst muttered to himself. He had expected him to be driving a car.

At low speed he followed him around a few corners until he reached the surgery. The doctor pulled up and got off. He secured the bike and removed the clips around his trouser legs, and as he took off his scarf Horst had a clear look at his face for the first time. He had built up a picture of him with glowering eyes and slightly vampiric teeth, but he looked like a nice, normal and even kind man. He wondered whether he had allowed himself to get over excited. Perhaps this wasn't going to be his big moment after all. He had to remind himself that he was a detective now, and it was his job to recognise that things were not always as they seemed. Maybe Irmgard had misunderstood the situation, or maybe she hadn't, but either way it was his job to find out.

'*Fortasse erit, fortasse non erit,*' he said to himself, a phrase that had returned to him from his schooldays. He remembered it meaning something like *Maybe, or maybe not.* He smiled. He had been hoping for something that would distinguish him from all the other renegade cops, with their drink problems, their vintage cars and their complicated jazz, and this would be it. He would be the one who muttered Latin phrases under his breath. As he waited for the doctor to reappear he sifted through his memory for one that might be an appropriate motto for his investigation. '*Fortuna favet fortibus,*' he muttered. He smiled. If he could only keep his nerve, and if fortune really did favour the brave, then this case could be his for the taking.

He took a sip of water, and waited.

VII

Madalena's train arrived in the city. The carriage had filled with commuters, and she waited for it to clear before taking her bag from the rack and stepping on to the platform. By the time she reached the concourse her fellow passengers had rushed away towards their jobs, and the place seemed deserted. She found a tourist information stand, and picked up a free city map. The street plan was surrounded by advertisements for taxi services, hotels and restaurants, but there was no mention of the museum. She scanned the map for a street name that matched the address on the clipping she had from the magazine. When she found it, hidden among the tangle of the Old Town, she memorised the landmarks and the turnings along the way.

Another train had arrived, and the station came to

life as its passengers stampeded towards the outside world. A minute later everything was quiet again, and it struck her how strange it was that tomorrow this would happen all over again – the same commuters would be rushing through the station, but she would be gone for ever. She walked outside. She could see her breath, and she shivered. Her jacket was too thin for the weather, but if anybody deserved to be cold it was her.

She looked at the lettering on the brass plate by the front door, and saw that the museum wouldn't be open for another hour and a half. She walked along the street, and not knowing what else to do she went into a coffee shop. When the man asked her what she would like, she was jarred by the unfamiliar sounds coming from his mouth. He asked again, in English, and she didn't understand this either, but the language of coffee was universal enough for her to end up with a mug in front of her. She handed over her ten euro note, waited for her change and found a seat.

Her thoughts kept returning to the woman who had offered her a banana all those trains ago, and she felt awful for not even having smiled at her. She had just shaken her head and looked away. She sipped her coffee, but only once. It sat in front of her, getting cold.

VIII

After three and a half hours the doctor left his clinic and cycled away. Horst followed him, and this time he parked alongside the house. He wound down his window, and listened. He heard a voice that he supposed belonged to the doctor, calling something that sounded like *Hans, fetch!* He wondered what this could mean, and then he heard what seemed to be a dog chasing a ball. 'Of course,' he said to himself, 'the hound in question.' After a bit more bouncing and rustling there was nothing, and just twenty-five minutes after the doctor had arrived back at his home he left again.

'*Tempus fugit*,' muttered Horst. He knew he would have to do better than that if his Latin-muttering trademark was to work. He had been struggling to remember phrases, and told himself that at the earliest opportunity he would go to the loft and find his old schoolbook. He made a note of the time, and beside it he wrote, *Suspect leaves house having exercised pet (dog), and perhaps eaten lunch.* He started the engine and once again drove behind the doctor, who at no point did anything other than cycle back to work.

He could see this was getting him nowhere. He wondered what his next move should be, and knew that whatever it was he would first have to stop worrying that his bladder was about to split open. He returned to the station and raced to the toilet, and when at last he could think straight he looked again at the Missing Persons files. No matter how many he read, he didn't feel any closer to a solution to what he had begun to think of as *The Irmgard Conundrum.*

Usually the person who had been reported missing would turn up alive and well, but sometimes a body would be found in the river or along a walking trail in the nearby hills. A few of them, though, were never seen again, and Horst had always been troubled by these unsolved cases. Every force had them, but still these files haunted him, and he would lie awake at night worried that he had failed in his duties, that he was missing a serial killer. He put the files away, and called his wife to tell her he was going to be late again.

'Horst?' she said, on hearing his voice. 'Horst, where are you? You promised to clean the rabbit hutch this morning. It's your turn. It's written on the calendar, right in front of me. Listen: *Horst to clean rabbit hutch in morning before work*. And now it's the afternoon. Honestly, Horst, I don't know what's come over you – you've become rather unreliable in recent hours.'

Horst remembered his commitment to clean the hutch, and felt a small burst of pleasure. This was the friction between work and home that a committed cop was supposed to feel. Even so, his wife had sounded particularly frosty, and on balance he supposed it would be best if he was to return home. 'Yes, dear,' he said. 'Sorry, dear. I shall be with you in eighteen minutes, but as soon as the hutch is clean I must return to work. Something quite important has come up.'

'You may do whatever you wish,' she snapped, 'as soon as you have done your chore.'

Horst brushed the little black pellets into a shovel, emptied them into a plastic bag and reached for fresh straw. 'What should I do now?' he asked.

The rabbits said nothing; they just carried on looking annoyed by all the upheaval. As he refreshed the water in their bottle, Horst could see that this business had gone on long enough. He resolved to pay the doctor a visit that evening, to listen to what he was certain would be an upsetting but very reasonable explanation of an unfortunate incident, and then leave him alone and return to his everyday duties. There would be no captured fiend, and no glory.

On his way out he passed his son as he returned

from school. Without thinking, he told him he was off
to catch a major criminal. His son wished him luck,
and as soon as he was out of the house Horst put his
hand to his brow, wondering what had led him to say
such a stupid thing.

IX

Madalena was on her third visit to Room Five, *Popular Methods*. She looked again at the razor blades and the pots of pills, the miniature railway, the scale model of a suspension bridge, the sawn-off shotgun and the largest exhibit in the museum – a real car with a hose running from its exhaust pipe to the rear window, a dummy slumped in the driver's seat. Beside each display was a card that listed some statistics and emphasised the possible consequences of failure. She couldn't read them, but she already knew how important it was to be sure that the end really would be the end. She could walk to any pharmacy counter and get pills, but she could never be sure that they would work; they might come straight back up having done her no harm at all, or leave her with agonising organ damage, or even brain injuries that would stop her from ever being able to correct her mistake. She knew she had to make it quick and effective.

The noose lay on its table, and she touched it. It was rough against her fingers, and it would be rough against her throat. She had already found the place to do it – a room in another part of the museum with a pipe running the length of the ceiling, and a table to stand on as she sets up the rope, and from which she will be able to jump.

There were hours left until the museum closed. She would have to leave and return later on. As she went from room to room one last time she was re-assured by all the photographs and the paraphernalia. So many people had done what she was about to do, and she was comforted by the idea that they would understand, that they wouldn't judge her. On the train, as she had pretended to sleep, she had pictured herself spending her last moments cold and alone, falling from a bridge into a fast-flowing river, dumb-bells tied to her wrists. Here in the museum it would feel as if she was spending these same moments among friends.

As she walked through the lobby her eyes caught those of the man behind the front desk, an old man with long, grey fingers. Hoping to compensate for her rudeness with the banana she attempted a smile but she couldn't make her lips move. It would have been for nothing anyway. He was already looking away.

★   ★   ★

She ordered another coffee from the same place. She sat at the same table, and after one sip she pushed the mug away. She had not felt thirsty or hungry since her drink with Mauro and Luciana, and she knew why that was: thirst and hunger are the body's way of saying that it needs to survive.

She took her pen and pad from her bag. Her mind was clearer than it had been on the train, and she could see she had been approaching the note from the wrong angle: it was not for her to express the complexity of her emotions, but to comfort the people she was leaving behind. The most important thing to do was reassure her mother and father that she had made the right decision, and that everybody will be better off when she has gone. She wanted them to know that it had been nobody's fault, and especially not theirs. She only touched on the way she felt, keeping her wording as straightforward as she could. As she wrote these sentences she hoped they wouldn't read them and think, *If it was only this darkness, if it was only this pain, if it was only this hatred of herself then we could have nursed her through it.* She told them she was beyond nursing, and beyond help, and she told them that she loved them, that she was sorry to have let them down this way, that she wished they could have had the daughter they deserved rather than the one they had ended up with. She told them they were not to feel sad for her, that they should be relieved to know that she is at last at peace.

She put the letter in the pocket of her jacket. She was sure that whoever was to find her would see that it got to them. She wondered if it would be the man with the long, grey fingers. She hoped it would be. He seemed like the kind of person who would understand.

X

The old man closed the front door and bolted it shut. Switching off lights as he went, he made his way upstairs and sat at the kitchen table. He cut himself a chunk of hardening cheese and a thin slice of bread. Looking straight ahead, he ate. The girl had returned, as he had known she would. He had come to recognise the signs. He could see from her eyes and from the way she held herself that there would be no drama, that he would be waking early in the morning and calling the doctor. There would be no need for him to interfere; all he had to do was let nature take its course.

When the food was gone he carried on sitting at the table, staring straight ahead. It was a quiet, still evening. Maybe if he listened hard enough he would be able to hear her heartbeat, or the soft shuffle of a spider's claws as it waited nearby.

Madalena lay behind the car in Room Five. When she was sure the old man had gone away she stood up and picked up the noose, and took it with her to the place she had chosen: Room Eight. She felt calm. She wasn't afraid of the dark, or of anything. Suddenly the room filled with light, and moments later the silence was shattered by a loud bang, like a gunshot. She went to the window. In the sky above the rooftops was a fading burst of colour. She had always enjoyed fireworks, but could no longer understand why.

She took the chair from the corner of the room and put it on the table. She knew she would need a long drop, but not so long that her feet would touch the floor. She climbed on to the table and on to the chair, and reached up to attach the rope with a single knot. Taking care not to make a noise, she climbed down and checked she had got it right. She had. Her feet would hang a few inches from the floor. She climbed back up, reinforced the knot and tested it by pulling on it with all her weight. It held firm. When the time comes she will stand on the edge and step forward, and she will fall, and it will all be over. For the first time in a long while she had something to look forward to.

Wanting to keep the inconvenience she was causing to a minimum, she put the chair back in the corner of the room. There was another flash, and a bang and a crackle. Her head was clear now. She was ready.

The old man was annoyed to hear these explosions. These were the test flares, final checks for the annual firework display at the castle. Every year he forgot about it until he heard these warning sounds. Soon it would all begin. He wished he had remembered to buy earplugs on his last trip out of the museum.

He changed into his nightshirt and nightcap, and pulled a Breton–German dictionary from the shelf. He lay on his bed, and read. *Nobl. Nobla. Noblañs*. As a long, grey finger traced a line beneath *Noblet*, his eyelids began to feel heavy. Voices carried up from the street, as people started making their way towards the castle grounds. He hoped he would not be kept awake by the commotion. He would have to be up early in the morning, and he didn't want his night's sleep to be curtailed at both ends.

XI

Horst pulled up outside the doctor's house. His palms were damp. He knew he was out of his depth, but he couldn't call his colleagues for help. On top of the humiliation of relinquishing the case there would be awkward questions about why he had kept such information to himself for so long. The only way was to carry on alone; if he was to turn up at the station with a scalp then these questions would not be asked. 'They will call me *The Lone Wolf*,' he mumbled.

There was a distant bang, and through the trees he saw a spray of light. He hadn't been looking for a sign, but if there was ever going to be one, this was it. Reminding himself of the motto he had given the investigation, he put on his cap and got out of the car.

He opened the side gate and walked up the doctor's driveway to his front door. A security light took him

by surprise, and from somewhere came the bark of a
dog. Making sure his cap was on straight, he rang the
bell. Moments later the door opened. The doctor was
already in his pyjamas.

'Doctor Fröhlicher?'

'Yes.'

'Doctor Ernst Fröhlicher?'

'Yes.'

'Doctor Ernst Fröhlicher . . . of this address?'

'Yes.'

'I wonder if I could have a moment to talk to
you about . . .' Horst wished he had prepared more
thoroughly. '. . . about a matter.'

'A matter?'

'Yes. A police matter.' He pointed to his cap.

'A police matter? Of course. Please go on.'

Horst stared directly at the doctor as he wondered
where to begin. Again he made sure his cap was on
straight.

The doctor looked concerned. 'Is this a matter of
urgency? Is a patient of mine in difficulty?'

Horst carried on staring. 'No,' he said. It was time
to drop the bombshell. He took a deep breath. 'I am
here to ask a few routine questions about the unexpected appearance of human body parts in the park.'

'Ah.' The doctor swallowed. He had been sure Frau
Klopstock would have kept this to herself. He was
angry with her for having gone to the police after
everything he had done for her over the years. His

mind raced as he thought of all the evidence he would have to destroy because of her. It was more than just *evidence* too; it was a large part of what made up his life. It all seemed such a waste. 'Of course, officer,' he said. 'I wonder if we could schedule an appointment for next week? Or perhaps the week after?' He smiled. 'Just like you, I am a very busy public servant.'

Horst's first instinct was to say *Yes doctor, that will be fine*, and go home for an early night, but he reminded himself that he was a tough cop now, and he said, quietly, 'No.'

The doctor visibly deflated, and Horst felt a surge of power, as if he was no longer playing a part. Without being invited, and in defiance of protocol, he entered the doctor's house. The door to the large open-plan living and dining room was open, and he went through. The doctor followed.

Horst supposed he should try to build up a rapport by making a little small talk. 'You have a very nice house, Doctor Fröhlicher,' he said.

'Please, call me Ernst,' said the doctor. 'Now, would you like a cup of coffee?'

Horst knew it would be a breach of police regulations to accept hospitality from a suspect, but even so he was tempted by the offer. He wondered whether this was yet another rule he should break. While he tried to resolve this inner conflict, he continued looking hard at the doctor, trying to connect the person he saw with the strangeness of the incident. He couldn't;

the doctor looked too much like a pleasant and normal man to have been involved in anything so unusual, and he wondered whether it was possible that Irmgard had been under a lot of strain and had only imagined the things she had supposedly seen in the park. After a long silence, Horst decided that *The Lone Wolf* must not be so easily swayed by appearances, and also that he must never accept a drink from a possible major criminal for fear of what it might contain. He said, quietly, 'No.'

'Very well,' said the doctor. 'Very well.'

Again, Horst was stuck for what to do next. It all seemed so implausible. He looked around at the room he was standing in. It was neat and orderly, but it seemed to lack something. He remembered what he had found out from Irmgard about the doctor's story; what was missing was any sign of family life. There were no feminine touches, and no scattered toys or trailing wires of video games, or any other evidence of a child or grandchild. He thought of the clutter of his own home, and was glad of it. He felt sorry for the doctor, but he knew he had to put his pity aside. He walked over to the dining table. On a plate was a partly eaten dome of brown meat. Knowing he had to break the silence, he spoke. 'This looks very tasty, doctor. What is it?'

The doctor slumped into an armchair. At first he hadn't known what to make of his visitor's unusual manner, but as their meeting progressed he had begun to feel the power of the policeman's unsettlingly long silences, and the penetrating stares that took in his every movement as he analysed even the slightest nuance of his body language. And now, his mind razor sharp, he had made his way straight to the evidence. There would be no use trying to fight somebody like this. They had sent their best man. It was over.

'Doctor? The meat?'

'You know what it is,' he said, quietly. He looked up, and their eyes locked. 'It is a buttock. A human buttock.'

Horst froze, but only for a moment. His heart thumped as he took out his notepad and pencil, and with trembling fingers he raced to keep up with the confession. His mind took a while to process what he was hearing, and it wasn't until the doctor was recounting the butchery and consumption of a third body that the scale and the nature of the crimes he had uncovered began to sink in. He felt his knees begin to buckle, but he steadied himself and carried on writing.

XII

The fireworks rattled the old man's window, and his thin, white curtains changed colour in the flashes of light. He lay still, his eyes fixed on the ceiling. In the castle grounds an orchestra was playing in time with the display, but the music didn't carry as far as the cold, bare rooms in the roof. When the first movement ended there was a round of applause then the evening fell quiet, but he knew the cacophony would soon return, and he wouldn't be able to sleep until it was over. His night already disrupted, he had no intention of waking up early in the morning as well.

He made a decision. When the second movement began he would go downstairs and see the girl. If necessary he would do as the doctor had requested, and help her on her way. By the time the fireworks were over he would be rid of her.

Madalena carried on looking at the small patch of sky above the rooftops, where the colour had been. Before she and Mauro had left for the city they had been to see the fireworks in their town, and as they stood side by side with their heads tilted back she had remembered how it had felt to be a little girl, and smiled at the thought that in years to come they would be there with children of their own. She had pictured a boy and a girl, their eyes sparkling as they looked up to the sky. These two had made regular appearances in her daydreams, and there in the museum she saw them again. This time they were farther away than usual, just beyond her reach.

'I'm sorry,' she said. She closed her eyes but they were still there, trusting her and loving her, seeming not to know that one evening, in a hotel bar with chandeliers and a white grand piano, she had let them down. 'I'm so sorry.' Smiling and laughing, they slipped out of focus, and faded away.

There was a rumble, and again the sky turned bright with fireworks. She wished she could make them stop, then it struck her that she *could* make them stop. She turned away from the window, and walked over to the table.

She climbed up, and put the noose around her neck. She tightened it, and closed her eyes.

XIII

As the doctor's confession continued, Horst became anxious. He knew he had to get him to the station so this monologue could continue within a recognised legal framework. The doctor was recounting some of the difficulties he had encountered while butchering a particularly plump young woman from Cloppenburg, and when this was finished he sighed, and Horst took this opportunity to say to him, 'Doctor, I wonder if we could continue this conversation in the comfort of the police station.'

The doctor thought for a moment, then sighed once again, and nodded. 'Yes, officer,' he said. 'I understand. But first I shall call my dog and say goodbye to him. He will be taken care of?'

Horst nodded. The dog would be taken care of, in a sense.

The doctor went over to the patio door and opened it, but instead of calling Hans he stood quietly for a moment, as if in contemplation, before running into the darkness. Horst, taken by surprise, raced out after him, to find that the doctor had tripped over a hosepipe, and was lying spread-eagled on the lawn. Before Horst could get to him he scrambled back on to his feet and ran to the high garden wall. He tried to climb over it, but ended up hanging by his fingers, his legs flailing, frog-like as his slippered feet failed to get a grip on the bricks. He gave up and stood in the flower-bed, bent double and panting. Through the still air came the crackle of fireworks.

'Very well,' he said. 'Very well.' The dog appeared, wagging his tail, and he followed the men back into the house.

Horst closed the patio door, and the doctor patted Hans. 'Somebody will be here to collect you, my friend,' he said. 'I'm so sorry.'

Leaving the dog locked in the house, the two men walked to Horst's car, the doctor's shoulders hunched. They got in, the doctor in the passenger seat. Horst was surprised by how calm he felt, knowing that in a few minutes he would be arriving back at the station with a soon-to-be-notorious cannibal. He smiled at the thought that Big Max Weber would be on the front desk. *Book him, Weber*, he will say, and Big Max Weber will ask what the charge is. He will leave a few moments before replying. Then he will smile and say, calmly,

Cannibalism. Big Max Weber was famously impassive. In moments of extreme surprise, though, he would raise his left eyebrow, and his colleagues had a running challenge to see if they could get him to do this. Horst had not managed it yet, but he had a feeling that tonight would be the night. This was his defining moment, the scalp of his career, and the biggest story the town had seen since he had joined the force. It was his *magnum opus.*

'*Magnum opus,*' he muttered under his breath. He looked forward to telling his son all about it.

As they got closer to the city centre the bangs became louder. People without tickets for the castle grounds were standing in clusters in spots where they could get a clear view of the display through the buildings and the trees.

'It is the fireworks tonight, Doctor Fröhlicher,' said Horst.

The doctor said nothing. He had decided that his story would not end this way. He was not ready to give up. He had thought of a plan, and in just a few seconds' time he would have a chance to carry it out.

XIV

Madalena stood on the table, her eyes closed and the noose tight around her neck. She pressed a hand against the pocket where she had put the note, making sure it was still there. It was. Now all she had to do was step forward. Not wanting to die with her eyes closed, she opened them and there in front of her, almost close enough to touch, was the old man, staring up at her. His nightshirt and nightcap were catching the flashes of colour from outside, while his face remained a deathly grey. She felt no surprise, or fear. She felt nothing. She looked back at him and he spoke, his voice barely audible above the noise from outside. She couldn't understand what he was saying.

'Don't try to save me,' she said.

She noticed what almost seemed to be the faintest flicker of a smile, then it vanished and he spoke to her in perfect Portuguese, in an accent that could have come from her own home town. 'I have not come to save you,' he said. 'I shall return in a short while, by which time I expect you to have finished what you have started.'

He turned and walked out of the room.

Madalena tried to put the old man out of her mind, and concentrate on her task. The whole encounter had been so strange it was almost as if it had never happened, but it had, and she had been unsettled by it. The fireworks thundered and crackled, and she closed her eyes again, and gathered herself in preparation. Once again, she was ready. She opened her eyes, and stepped forward.

Before her back foot left the table, she stopped. She could smell something. It was wonderful. She opened her eyes, and looked around her. She was no longer ready. She was no longer calm. She realised she was alone in a foreign land, in a place where she wasn't meant to be, with a noose around her neck and one foot suspended in the air. The second movement stopped, and the city fell quiet. She was terrified.

XV

It happened so fast. The car stopped at a red light, and the doctor unclipped his seat belt and opened the door. Horst made a lunge to restrain him, but reined in by his own seat belt he managed only to get a grip on the doctor's elasticated waistband. With a few kicks, a wriggle and a forward roll on to the street, the doctor was free. He ran off, leaving Horst gaping at the pyjama trousers in his hand. A moment later, abandoning the car in the middle of the road and not even stopping to close the door, Horst got out and gave chase.

As he ran, he could feel his big moment slipping away. Instead of making Big Max Weber raise an eyebrow, he would have to explain to his son that he had lost his job by letting the city's biggest ever criminal slip from his grasp. He pictured the look on his wife's face as they packed their belongings into crates, getting ready to leave town in disgrace. It was chilling. Even the rabbits looked disappointed in him. Spurred on by his need to avoid this outcome, and keeping his eyes fixed firmly on the retreating bare bottom, he ran. Already he was short of breath, and there was tightness in his chest, but he didn't slow down.

The doctor ran into the maze of pedestrianised streets in the city centre, looking for an opportunity to shake off his pursuer. He caught the occasional glimpse of himself in a shop window and wished he was wearing something on his bottom half, but he didn't have time to dwell on it. One of his slippers had fallen from his foot as he made his escape, and he hopped along for a few paces as he balanced things out by kicking off the other one. The pavement scraped against his bare soles with every stride, but while he was aware of the discomfort he focused only on getting away. He knew exactly where he was going. Once he had shaken off the policeman he would make his way to the back of the museum and rouse the old man, who would have no choice but to take him in and give him trousers, and hide him from those who would lock him away. They would live together in the roof. He would have to share his meat from now on, but that was a small price to pay for relative freedom, and besides the old man didn't look as though he had much of an appetite. Maybe they would even have a stroke of good fortune that night, and be eating a supper of fresh steak before bedtime.

The people standing in the streets were craning their necks to see the flashes of light, but every so often one of them would notice him streak past. Already in a carnival mood they laughed at the sight, and nudged their friends and pointed. It was only the adults with young children who looked on with horror as his private parts, no longer private, windmilled as he ran. Occasionally he would weave around somebody who would think, *That man looks just like Doctor Fröhlicher. I must remember to tell him about this the next time I see him – he will be very amused.*

The doctor looked over his shoulder at the purple-faced policeman chasing him, and was angered by the advantage the other man's shoes gave him over his own bare feet. Everything about this situation seemed unfair, but what irked him most of all was that he was so clearly morally superior to those who would condemn him. He looked at the people he was running past, and knew they would be horrified if they had known what he had done, that they would label him a *monster*, or a *fiend*, but he knew in his heart that he had done so much more good than harm in his life, that on balance he was a better person than any of them would ever be. He was a doctor, and though there was no way of quantifying the good he had done, he knew it was considerable, even when his occasional transgressions were taken into account. He looked at those who would denounce him, and could see that they were just ordinary people who cared little about anything beyond the boundaries of their own lives, people who drank normal coffee without giving a thought to the lives of those who produced it. He knew just by looking at them that they lived only to look after themselves, and to cast judgement on others. As anger burned inside him he longed to throw back his head and shout *Hypocrites*, but he didn't. He just kept running, as fast as he could. He didn't want to draw attention to himself.

The policeman was gaining ground. There were only a few paces between them but he was no longer worried. His chance to shake him off had come at last. He was approaching the gardens surrounding the City Hall, and all he had to do was scale the high fence and disappear into the darkness around the back of the building. With so many possible points of exit he knew the policeman would have no idea which one he had taken. With an athletic bound he jumped up and gripped the black iron railings, and feeling as agile as a monkey he made it to the top. As he vaulted over, his hand slipped and his body fell, landing on the long spikes. For a moment it felt as if this wouldn't matter, that he would be able to lift himself off and keep going, but he couldn't. The cold metal dug into his flesh, and the spikes broke the surface of his skin. He counted four holes, from his chest to his abdomen. His strength had left him, and the agony registered only as an irrelevance. The usefulness of pain had passed; it told him nothing he didn't already know. In his mind he charted the passage of the spikes as they penetrated organs, and cracked bones. They pushed against the skin of his back, then broke it, and he slipped down until he could go no further. He tried to see himself as an impaled martyr, misunderstood and hounded to his doom by his fellow men, but the elaborate speeches of self-justification he had planned for his final moments, the words that had seemed so noble, vanished from his mind.

The policeman was looking up at him.

Horst could see that this would be his last opportunity to question the doctor. Something had been bothering him as they were running through the streets. His confession had seemed quite comprehensive, but at no point had the doctor mentioned how he had got hold of the bodies he had butchered. Horst knew that if he was going to claim true glory he would have to find this out. 'Did you work alone?' he asked.

The doctor's high ideas left him, and his humanity took over. He felt only a desire to share the blame, to drag somebody else down with him. He looked at the policeman, and said, 'I had an accomplice. He lives at the museum . . .' Then the policeman vanished, and everything around him vanished until he was no longer stuck on the railings of the City Hall on a cold evening, but standing in a lovely garden on a clear summer day, and there before him was Ute.

'Ute,' he said, 'you look beautiful.' Her eyes had

never been bluer, her hair more golden or her smile so sweet. Then her blue eyes narrowed, and her smile turned cold. He reached out to touch her, but she was gone. And then everything was gone.

Horst bent double, and struggled to recover his breath. It was time to call for help. He took his phone from his pocket, and as he continued gasping he saw that his wife had sent him a message. He supposed he had better read it before doing anything else. *It is lucky for you that we do not have a dog*, he read, *because if we did your dinner would be inside it by now*. He would call her and explain, but first he had to contact the station and ask for urgent reinforcements and an ambulance to be sent as quickly as possible. Soon a small crowd had gathered around him. They stared at the body on the railings, knowing this would be the only time in their lives when they would get to see such a sight. They didn't want to look away, not even for a moment. Horst searched for an appropriate Latin phrase to mutter, but none came to mind.

The people stared and stared, oblivious to the fireworks as they built to a crescendo, and seeming not to hear the sirens, distant at first, but growing louder all the time.

XVI

The unexpected aroma had gone away. For a moment, though, it had overwhelmed her, and for the first time in days she felt hungry, even ravenous. Her eyes were closed as the firework display's finale shook the table and then stopped, leaving the room still and quiet. A moment later there was a wave of applause, and she wished she had been there to see it properly, that she was one of the people clapping in the cold air. The rope was tight against her throat, and she knew she had to take it off and get away. She opened her eyes, and through the darkness she saw that the old man had returned. A fire extinguisher stood beside him on the floor.

'This has gone on long enough,' he said. 'You have made your decision. Allow me to assist.' He walked to the table, took hold of the back corner and tipped it forwards. Madalena's feet slid down the tabletop, and in a panic she turned and kicked on the corner he was lifting, forcing him to drop it back into place. Straightaway he took hold of it again, but she stamped hard on his long, grey fingers. She looked at his face, and where she had thought there would be anger there was nothing. He walked to the fire extinguisher, and picked it up. She could see now why he had brought it with him. She tried desperately to loosen the noose. Just minutes ago she had been sure she had nothing to live for, but now she was struggling harder than she had ever struggled for anything. The old man lifted the fire extinguisher over his shoulder, and swung it hard at her legs.

She was powerless against this blow. It knocked her off the table. She hadn't quite been able to get the noose off, and as she fell it caught against her chin, jolting her head backwards before swinging free. She landed hard on the floor, and looked up. There it hung, empty. She could still hear the applause, and for that moment she felt it was for her. The old man was glaring at her, and now there seemed to be a hint of fury in his eyes. The fire extinguisher was still in his hands, and he walked towards her and lifted it high. As he brought it down hard she rolled away, and it hit the floor where a fraction of a second earlier her head had been. It slipped from his grip, and Madalena took hold of it, stood up, and swung it at him. She had aimed for his head but its weight pulled it down, and it hit him in the side. He staggered, and she swung it again, this time catching him in the belly. He fell. She lifted her weapon high, and was ready to smash it down into his face when a weak, pitiful sound came from his mouth.

'No,' he said. 'Please. Please, no.'

There was fear in his eyes now, real fear, and she didn't know what to do.

'There is no need,' he said, still in the accent that could have come from home. She knew she couldn't trust him, but at the same time she didn't want to batter a frightened old man to death. She didn't know what to do. She had no idea how to get out of the building, and if she was to run he might come after her. He would know every inch of the museum, and there would be nowhere to hide. She carried on wielding the fire extinguisher as he stood up and went to the corner of the room, where he picked up the wooden chair. He took it over to the table, and using it as a step he climbed up, and put Madalena's noose over his head. If his time had come to die, he would rather it was by his own hand than by hers.

The old man had never had a great deal of interest in living, but no matter how often he told himself that he was not afraid of death, he had always known he could never end his own life. He had been certain that if he was ever to come close his survival instinct would be just as strong as that of the spiders as they thrashed around inside his mouth, frantic as they tried to delay their final moments. Sometimes as he crushed their soft bodies between his teeth, he wondered what made them fight so hard. Was it the webs left unspun? Or maybe lodged somewhere inside their tiny brains was an inescapable dread of what might lie beyond.

He had always found the people who had died in the museum to be a profound irritation, mainly because of the inconvenience they caused him and the threat they posed to the continuing stillness of his day-to-day life, but also because they awoke in him an ungovernable jealousy for having risen above the spiders. He wished he could conquer his fear of the possibility that he had been wrong to put his faith in nothingness, that perhaps he really was something more than a tangle of atoms, that the end would not be the end and there would be unbearable consequences awaiting him. Now, though, it seemed his time had come, and he was ready to find out. He tightened the rope.

'God forgive me,' he said, just in case it was to make a difference, but as the words came out he knew he wouldn't be able to go through with it. He wasn't ready. All he wanted was to get his days back to the way they had been, and the way he wanted them to stay. The girl had given him the opportunity to gather his thoughts. Now he knew that the only thing he could do was finish what he had started, and call the doctor and haul her lifeless body through the fire exit and into the back of the car. When that was done he would never have to think of her again. He lifted his hands and loosened the rope.

Madalena could see what he was doing. She wasn't going to give him another chance to come after her, and she swung the fire extinguisher at his legs. The old man fell from the table, and he hung from the pipe, rocking just a little from side to side, his eyes seeming to stare at her as they bulged from their sockets. His mouth hung open, and Madalena noticed a thin leg emerging from the darkness, and then another. The spider rested on the old man's bottom lip, black against the grey skin. For just a moment it remained perfectly still, as if considering its next move. Then, its decision made, it ran down the nightshirt and on to the floor, and into the safety of the shadows.

Madalena grabbed her bag and ran into the corridor, and down the stairs, and in and out of dark rooms until she found the fire exit. She pushed it open and slammed it behind her, and hurried along the dim, deserted back alley to the street. It was packed with happy people who had been to the fireworks, and she let herself be swept along with them, but soon she broke away to look at her reflection in a mirror in a shop window display. She tidied her hair, and checked her throat. There were some red marks. Until they faded she would have to wear a scarf, but for now she turned up the collar of her coat. As the adrenaline drained away she felt first the cold, and then pain. Her neck was stiff from her chin having caught on the rope, and there were going to be bruises on her legs, and her arms hurt from swinging the fire extinguisher. None of this mattered.

She had never been so thirsty, or so hungry. She walked on until she found a shop selling food and drink. She bought a two-litre bottle of water and a loaf of bread. She sat on a wall and watched the thinning crowd pass by as she began her picnic. She drank most of the water in one go, then opened the paper bag and brought it to her nose. She inhaled. It was just normal bread, like any of the loaves she had eaten since leaving her village. She couldn't imagine the scent of bread like this ever travelling hundreds of miles and overwhelming the senses of an unhappy girl, and calling her home. She took a bite. It tasted just as ordinary as it smelled. But, for now, it would do.

PART FIVE

I

Doctor Fröhlicher's patients woke to a brief item on the regional news, telling them that their general practitioner had been impaled on the railings of the City Hall gardens, and had died at the scene. This was met with quiet disbelief and profound sorrow. The universal assumption was that he must have slipped while trying to get a good view of the fireworks. The police had decided to wait before releasing any further details, but with the house sealed off and clearly under intense forensic examination, the local reporters could see that there was more to the story than they were being told.

The police had to say something, and at midday a statement was issued, confirming the reports that the deceased had been found in a state of undress after a chase through the streets, and announcing the unexpected news that his garage had housed several suspicious freezers. They held off from mentioning the discovery of body parts, but they did let the reporters know that one of these freezers contained a frozen cat that was being tested for evidence of human sexual interference.

When his patients heard this, they shook their heads and sighed. *What a shame*, they said to one another. *What a shame that the doctor's private life is being made public in this way, and with him no longer around to present his side of the story.* Nobody said it out loud, but each of them asked themselves whether they could put their hand on their heart and say with absolute certainty that if they had been in the doctor's position they would not, in a moment of desolation, have had sex with a frozen cat.

It was not until the afternoon that the police felt ready to announce that they had strong evidence to suggest that extensive cannibalism had taken place on the premises. At this point the story exploded, but even as the town filled with news crews from around the world, the doctor's patients continued to give him the benefit of the doubt. They stayed tuned to their radios, waiting for a newscaster to tell them that the police had found the *real* culprit, and that the poor man could at last rest in peace, but with each new bulletin a fresh piece of evidence was revealed, and one by one they began to consider the possibility that there had been more to their doctor than had met the eye.

Among those listening to the radio were Franz and

Irmgard Klopstock. The incident in the park had allowed them some time to prepare for these revelations, but even so they listened in dismay as their very worst fears were confirmed. After dinner they were interrupted by the doorbell, and they answered it to find Horst. It was the first time they had seen him since Irmgard had given her statement, and he looked as though he hadn't stopped since. His hair was sticking up in tufts, and there was a growth of stubble on his pale face, but although it was clear that he needed a good night's sleep, his eyes were bright.

The city's Chief of Police was notoriously formidable, but when Horst had been called into his office that afternoon he had never seen him quite so incandescent. He was sitting behind his enormous desk with a list of *The Lone Wolf*'s misdemeanours in his hand, his face turning increasingly crimson as he read out each one. When at last he reached the end he slammed the list on to the table, looked him in the eye, and told him that if he ever stepped out of line again he would be out of the force.

'Do you understand?' he snarled.

'Yes, sir,' said Horst. He had been waiting his whole career for this scene. For years he had pictured his superior giving him a stern dressing down, even though they both knew that it was just a formality, that under the skin they were two of a kind, each as committed as the other to cleaning vermin off the streets, even if it meant bending the rules from time to time. But instead of basking in an atmosphere of tacit mutual respect, he felt like a schoolboy being told off by his headmaster, and as he watched the veins in the Chief's temples throb with such violence it seemed they would burst, he felt as if his knees were turning to jelly. He made to leave, but was called back.

'Not so fast,' the Chief snapped. Horst faced him once again, and saw the faintest trace of a smile playing across his lips as he tore the list into pieces, and dropped them in the bin. 'Good work,' he said, quietly. His snarl returned. 'Now get out.'

It was perfect.

In between sips of Irmgard's home-made gooseberry juice, Horst brought his hosts up to date with what had happened since they had last met, trusting them with details that had yet to be made public. He told them about the stake-out, the arrest and the chase, and the subsequent discovery of diaries and photograph albums that detailed everything the doctor had been up to. He had reached the real reason for his visit. He put on his cap, and took a deep breath.

'As you now know, Doctor Fröhlicher was a man of many peculiarities, one of which, I am sorry to say, was an extensive collection of photographs of mal-functioning anuses. Frau Klopstock, it doesn't give me any pleasure to tell you that among these photographs are many close-ups of an anus that is very clearly labelled as belonging to you. In fact it has an entire album to itself. I have seen it, as have many of my colleagues. I hate to be the one to tell you that these pictures leave absolutely nothing to the imagination.'

Irmgard buried her face in her hands. For the first time since all this had begun she gave in to sobs. Franz placed a hand on her trembling shoulder, and gave it a squeeze.

'I would rather you heard it from me than from a news bulletin,' said Horst. They all looked at the radio, which had been switched off.

Irmgard nodded, and sniffed. 'Thank you, officer,' she whispered. 'You are very kind.'

'It looked rather painful,' he said. 'I do hope you're on the mend.'

She nodded once again. 'I've completely recovered in that department. But tell me,' she said, changing the subject to one that had been troubling her all day, 'what about poor Hans? What will become of him?'

'Hans is being kept at the police pound. He is being well-fed and regularly exercised, and in seven days' time, in accordance with standard procedure, he will be shot dead.'

'But, Horst . . .' She checked herself. 'But, *officer*, that dear dog . . .' Irmgard put her hand to her mouth as she remembered the times she had seen him running in the park, how happy he had been, and how good-natured. 'What if he was to find a loving home?'

Horst took off his cap and shook his head. 'I am

afraid, Irmgard, that he is already being referred to as *The Cannibal Hound*. If anybody is interested in taking him in they are more likely to be ghoulish souvenir hunters than dog lovers. It would be impossible to know if he is going to a good home. Trust me, Irmgard, this is the kindest way. It will be a single bullet to the back of his head as he chews on a bone. He won't know it's coming, and he won't feel a thing.'

'But, Horst,' she said. 'Franz and I have been talking. Perhaps we could . . .' She looked at Franz, and smiled. Franz smiled back. '. . . perhaps Hans could come and live here, with us?'

'Even after everything you saw in the park?'

Irmgard nodded.

'I'm afraid that would be impossible.'

Irmgard looked at the carpet.

'Is there really nothing you can do?' asked Franz.

Horst thought for a while. 'Well,' he said, 'under the circumstances, I might be able to pull some strings . . .' He was quite often placed on routine duties at the pound. He had the keys, and was familiar with all the paperwork. He thought for a while longer. Maybe *The Lone Wolf* had one final howl left in him. 'Perhaps we could discreetly arrange a new identity for him. We could change his name to . . .' He stroked his bristly chin, then smiled. '. . . Hansel.'

Irmgard stood up and fetched her coat. 'Well, what are we waiting for?' she said. 'Let's bring him home. Let's bring Hansel Klopstock home.'

The three of them went out to Horst's car.

As Horst pulled on his seatbelt he thought of a joke to lighten the sombre mood that had taken hold. 'Of course you realise you will have to change the dog's diet just a little?' He was pleased with this, and his passengers were too.

Smiling, they drove away.

II

Within two hours of the doctor's death, the police had retrieved a log of phone calls to and from his home number, and following Horst's tip-off about a museum connection they had read enough of his diaries to have a good idea that something untoward had been going on between him and the old man. Sirens blazing, they raced to the scene, where they battered their way in through the front and back doors.

He was where Madalena had left him, his eyes wide open, as if he was watching them. Being taller than her, his feet had grazed the floor as he fell. His neck had not broken, and his toes had taken enough of his weight for his blood flow to be stemmed, but it had not stopped.

He was cut down and taken to the hospital, where they dressed him in white and placed him under a white sheet. Food and water entered his grey body through a tube, and his breathing was assisted by a machine that made a low undulating drone.

Tests showed that significant parts of his brain had stopped functioning. There was no possibility of him regaining consciousness, but his heart was beating as it always had. When asked how long he could be expected to live like this, the doctor in charge said it was impossible to predict, but that there was every possibility he could go on for many years to come.

He shrugged. 'Maybe he will outlive us all.'

The old man lay still, thinking of nothing. As his chest rose and fell, the machine rumbled on. In and out, in and out. It all sounded the same.

III

Pavarotti longed for his sedated wife to wake up so he could offer her words of consolation, but at the same time he was struggling to think what those words would be. Leaving her in the care of a nurse, he went out of the house, hoping the fresh air would clear his head. He walked through dark streets until he reached the museum. The press had not yet been tipped off about the building's connection to the doctor, but its lights were on and a policeman had been discreetly placed near the battered front door. The policeman recognised Pavarotti, and didn't ask him to move along when he sat on the steps.

Pavarotti's mind was just as blank as it had been at home, and when he heard a bright *Good evening,* and looked up to see Hulda, he was glad of the company. She too had spent the day with the police, and there had been an inevitability to the route of her own head-clearing walk. After everything they had heard they both felt as if they didn't know the museum at all, and they had each felt driven to go there again, to see if it was as they remembered it, and even to double-check that it had ever existed at all. It had been an exhausting time, and they knew there would be more questions in the morning. She sat beside him.

'What a shame about Herr Schmidt,' she said.

Pavarotti nodded.

'It's terrible, isn't it? All those poor people being eaten like that.'

'It's a shame for you too, Hulda,' said Pavarotti. 'I fear you will soon be looking for alternative employment.'

Hulda sighed. 'All good things must come to an end. You don't have to worry about me though – I'm sure my probation officer will find me something suitable before too long.' With this she began recounting the highlights of her long day. She had been woken early by a knock at the door, and the unexpected news, and after getting dressed she had been taken to the police station. She had recognised a lot of the people working on the case, and they had greeted her warmly. *Hello, Hulda*, they said, *it's good to see you again*. They treated her just as well as they had the last time, bringing her coffee and snacks, and making sure she was comfortable. Some of them joked that if it hadn't been for her they would be out of a job. There had been moments when it had been like catching up with old friends.

One Saturday morning when she was still a school-girl, and while her mother was at the market, Hulda's stepfather had padded up behind her as she tidied the kitchen. He grabbed her. She felt his moustache rub against her cheek. She had lost count of the times this had happened, but this was the first time she had *wanted* him to grab her, to rub himself against her, and to say, *You know what to do.* She caught a vicious blast of pickle-breath, and it felt good, it was what she had been hoping for. She was impatient for him to unzip his trousers, and she didn't have to wait long.

It poked from his body, this pinkish-grey stamen of which she had once been so petrified, and she looked at it and looked back at him, and took it in her hand as she had so many times before. Without a trace of fear she used her other hand to reach for the knife that she had been sharpening for days in anticipation of this moment, and with a single movement that she had practised on carrot after carrot, and on parsnip after parsnip, she made sure he would never be able to do his damage again, not to her, not to her mother, not to anybody. He fell screaming to the floor, his hands cupped around the bloody stump. She had heard about surgeons who could reattach these things, and she needed to be sure that would not happen. She dropped the gristly lump on to the tiles and stamped on it again and again, until she could see it was beyond repair. Just to be sure, she picked it up and sawed it in half, from tip to base. He tried to get up and stop her, to grab it and keep it safe, but the agony and the threat of the knife drove him back down. Only when she knew she had destroyed it did she call for help. Just in case he had ideas of revenge or escape she pressed the blade hard against his throat as they waited for the ambulance to arrive.

When they had taken him away, and she sat at the kitchen table surrounded by police, she realised the extent of what she had done. Her mind was clear, and she told them everything. She had no regrets for having ended things the way she had, and nor would she ever. She knew in her heart that she had done the right thing, and she would never say sorry.

She had not been sent to jail, but the authorities knew that they couldn't simply let her go about her business after what she had done, particularly after her refusal to even feign regret, and since then her life had been filled with criminal psychologists, counsellors and rehabilitation officers, all of whom had grown very fond of her.

As Hulda and Pavarotti sat together on the cold steps of the museum she felt as if their shared involvement in this latest calamity had brought down the social barriers that had stood between them, and for the first time she was ready to make friendly conversation with him.

'Has anybody ever told you that you look just like Pavarotti?' she asked.

He told her, quite truthfully, that nobody had.

As they sat in silence, Hulda felt something building inside her, a sense that with this new-found rapport had come one of the big moments of her life, an opportunity she could not let pass her by. She felt a surge of confidence, and as calm as anything, she said, 'I've been wondering if you have a brother.'

Pavarotti looked a little taken aback as he nodded. 'Yes,' he said. 'I do.'

'And are you at all similar?'

'He's like me in many ways, although he doesn't have one of these . . .' He pointed.

'He doesn't have a face?' Hulda was overcome with pity.

'No, I mean he doesn't have a beard.'

She was relieved, and her courage returned. She ploughed on before it had a chance to get away. 'And is he married?'

'No. No, I'm afraid to say that's another way in which we differ. Unlike me, he is unlucky in love. He was engaged for a time, but for one reason or another he and his fiancée never quite made it to the church.'

The idea of Pavarotti's brother was making Hulda's blood run hot with passion. 'Is he younger than you, or older?'

'He is older.' Hulda had been hoping for the other answer, but if happiness lay in the arms of a man of advanced years then she would still be glad of it. She wondered just how old he was, and as if reading her mind, Pavarotti continued. 'He's twenty-nine.'

Hulda was amazed. She looked at Pavarotti, and for the first time she saw that he was not a great deal older than she was. The skin around his eyes was smooth and fresh. The years that had only ever been assumptions melted away, and she felt a little ashamed, but this soon passed. 'I think it would take our minds off the terrible events if you were to call him,' she said. 'Will you call him now, and invite him to meet us?'

Pavarotti was no longer baffled by Hulda's interrogation. Since they were no longer going to be professionally connected he saw no reason why he shouldn't make this introduction. He did as she had asked, and after a short conversation he hung up. 'He's on his way. He lives forty minutes from here.'

Hulda was experiencing urges she had only ever imagined, and she told herself she was going to yield to them at the first opportunity. It wouldn't happen that night, but it would happen soon. She didn't care what God thought; for once in His life He could keep his nose out of her business.

They stood up, and as they walked away a police van pulled up, and uniformed officers got out and started taping off the building. Hulda and Pavarotti made their way along the narrow street as men with large cameras raced past them, hoping to get the first photographs of this second House of Horrors.

With Pavarotti by her side, and knowing she was about to meet his brother, Hulda felt a sense of harmony with the world that she had not known since she had been a little girl, and in a flash she realised she wasn't necessarily going to Hell after all. God would have known the trouble that had been in her heart on the night she had let Him down, just as He must have known how sincere her apologies had been. She had forgiven her mother when she admitted that deep down she had suspected her husband had been mistreating her for all those years, but she had been so frightened of the man that she had managed to convince herself that nothing was wrong. 'I'm sorry, Hulda,' she had said, and Hulda had known she meant it, and had forgiven her straight away. She had even forgiven her stepfather when they had met on an organised prison visit some months after his trial. He had sat before her, a broken, cockless man, and told her how sorry he was for everything he had done to her. If she could forgive them but God still wouldn't forgive her, then . . . She didn't know what to think. Everything seemed so new. She was shaken from her thoughts by Pavarotti.

'In my younger days I would very occasionally go to a bar just around the corner,' he said. 'Let's see if it's still there.'

They walked on, side by side.

IV

The railway line met the highway, and for a while they ran parallel. Madalena was relieved to see signs pointing to places she had heard of. A billboard was advertising toothpaste, and Mauro's smile was as dazzling as ever. She checked her phone and found a message from him, telling her that he was halfway up Mount Fuji in a white tuxedo, and asking if she and João were still on for meeting up when he got back. She texted her reply, telling him, just truthfully enough, that the João thing hadn't really worked out, so it would only be the three of them. She said she was looking forward to it, and she meant it. It would be good to see him, and to get to know Luciana better.

Everything seemed so clear now. She had let him go, and it had been the right thing to do, and though it had been difficult she had got through it. She had survived. For so many years she hadn't been able to imagine life without him, but now she was living that life, and she was going to be fine. Like a teenage girl taking down an old poster of a pop star, she was moving her life forward, and growing up. She was being realistic, understanding that happiness, true happiness, lay elsewhere. She had a sense that she was finding her place in the world, and it felt good.

She had slept for hours, first in a cheap hotel in the city and then in short bursts on train after train as she made her way home. Only ghosts of feelings remained, and it seemed as if the whole episode had happened to somebody else, that she had only been an observer. She would be able to recount what she had done, action by action, but she would never be able to articulate the unbearable feelings that had been inside her all that time. Language had let her down again, but this time it didn't matter.

They left the road behind, and the train carried on through farmland. She put her hand in her pocket and pulled out the note she had written. She unfolded it, and as she read it her new-found calm drained away and she was frightened of herself. It no longer felt as if it had been somebody else's experience: this was *her* handwriting, and these were *her* words. She could see how sincere she had been, and how ready, and how blind. She had truly believed that her mother and father would have found comfort in this letter, that they would have accepted her assurance that she had been beyond help. She had really thought that they would be glad to know she was *at peace,* whatever that was supposed to mean. She hadn't been able to see that the rest of their lives would have been ruined, blighted by the thought that they had let her down. She could see that she had been out of her mind, and had been convinced that there was no possibility of ever finding a way through the darkness. If she hadn't been interrupted by the old man, if he hadn't stirred her fears and doubts and cleared the way for a spark of hope to reach her through the chaos, then she would have gone through with it.

She folded the letter. She would keep it, for a while at least, to remind herself of just how wrong it was possible to be.

The train slowed as it entered the city, and she got her bag down from the rack. She took the bus back to her room, where she changed her clothes, and showered, and once again packed clean things for a night or two away. She lay down on her bed, and as she closed her eyes she saw the little boy and the little girl from her daydreams. They were the same as they had ever been. They were smiling, and loving her, and trusting her.

In the morning she would go to the bus station, and finish her journey.

V

It is already dark by the time her bus gets in. As a huddle of old people stand in the shadows and watch, she gets off and walks in the direction of the shops. Her eyes are fixed on the pavement, and whenever she sees a piece of gravel in the light of a streetlamp she reaches down and picks it up. She doesn't worry for a moment that he will have done as she had asked, and found somebody else to love. He will be there.

She stands outside the bakery, and looks up. She knows which window is his. Everybody knows his window. It is dark, and closed against the cold air, and the curtain is pulled across, but this is what she has been expecting. The next day is market-day, and he will have gone to bed in anticipation of an early start. She takes a piece of gravel between her fingers, and throws it at the glass. She has a good aim. It bounces off, and the window remains dark. She throws another piece, and nothing happens. She throws another, and another, and she begins to worry, but then a hand appears, and the curtain opens. A face looks down at her, and her confidence drains away. She feels shy, and nervous, in ways she has never felt before, and she wonders if she is making a mistake by standing in the street with a handful of gravel.

Moving from shadow to shadow, the old people had followed her as she walked through the town. From a dark spot along the street they look on as the window opens, and the bare-footed young baker climbs down the drainpipe. For a moment it looks as if neither the boy nor the girl knows what to do, but then they start to talk. Their voices are quiet, little more than whispers, and the old people are too far away and too hard of hearing to make out any of the words, but they can see that they have a lot to say to one another, and that their conversation is a serious one. The young baker and the girl move underneath a streetlamp, and they don't know why but she takes off her scarf and he gently runs his fingers across her throat. He reaches down and takes her hand. They talk for a while longer, then he takes her other hand and pulls her close, and wraps his arms around her as she rests her head on his shoulder.

The old people look on as he places his hands on either side of her face, and they can see that she is smiling. He kisses her lips, not with the awkwardness that they would have expected, but as if it is the most natural thing in the world. One by one they drift away, back to their families to tell them the news. In kitchens and parlours across the town, sticks are waved in the air, and the announcement made that the sun will no longer be setting to the mournful sound of a dented euphonium.